Ed

"I'm sorry for not telling everyone that you were nowhere near the Logan property when it caught on fire..."

Kara took a ragged breath, voice quavering as her tear-filled eyes sought his. "Can you ever forgive me?"

"Already did, darlin'," his low voice assured her. "A long time ago."

She stared at him. Not comprehending the kindness reflected in his eyes.

"I knew you were scared." His words washed over her in a reassuring wave. "Understood why you didn't want anyone to know you were with me."

"I'm so sorry. I hate myself for what you had to go through."

"No need for that." His eyes grew thoughtful as if mentally traveling back in time.

She clenched her fists in an effort to warm ice-cold fingers. To stop their trembling.

"It's all in the past." Gentle eyes echoed his smile. "Let's leave it there."

Wonder filled her. "Thank you. But you never liked this town, even before the fire. Why did you come back?"

He smiled at her. "Guess you might call it unfinished business."

Books by Glynna Kaye

Love Inspired

Dreaming of Home
Second Chance Courtship

GLYNNA KAYE

treasures memories of growing up in small Midwestern towns—in Iowa, Missouri, Illinois—and vacations spent in another rural community with the Texan side of the family. She traces her love of storytelling to the many times a houseful of great-aunts and -uncles gathered with her grandma to share hours of what they called "windjammers"—candid, heartwarming, poignant and often humorous tales of their youth and young adulthood.

Glynna now lives in Arizona, and when she isn't writing she's gardening and enjoying photography and the great outdoors.

Second Chance Courtship
Glynna Kaye

Steeple
Hill®

Published by Steeple Hill Books™

STEEPLE HILL BOOKS

Steeple
Hill®

Recycling programs
for this product may
not exist in your area.

ISBN-13: 978-0-373-81532-6

SECOND CHANCE COURTSHIP

www.SteepleHill.com

Printed in U.S.A.

I run in the path of your commands,
for you have set my heart free.
—*Psalms* 119:32

To my sister and best friend, Sheryl,
who faithfully reads all my drafts—
and never complains even during
the third or fourth round.

ACKNOWLEDGMENTS

Thank you again to Steeple Hill Love Inspired
senior editor, Melissa Endlich,
for enthusiastically allowing me
to share Canyon Springs with the world.

Thanks also to my agent, Natasha Kern, for her
words of encouragement and vote of confidence.

And as always, an extra special
thank-you to my "Seeker Sisters"
at www.Seekerville.blogspot.com.
I'm still amazed at how
God brought us all together.

Chapter One

Cowboys ain't nothin' but trouble.

The oft-heard parental warning echoed through Kara Dixon's head. No surprise, for in the dim light and blowing snow outside a Canyon Springs, Arizona, restaurant, her eyes had fastened on the back of a broad-shouldered, dark-haired specimen of the cowboy variety. The Western hat and shearling jacket might be mimicked by wannabes, but the horse trailer hitched behind a big, silver Ford pickup vouched for his authenticity.

A cowboy. Yet another reason she had to get out of this town and back to Chicago. The sooner the better, too. She'd yet to run into a bona fide wrangler on the streets of the Windy City, which suited her just fine.

But how could she not take pity on the poor man? A man who valiantly endeavored to hand-brush fast accumulating snow from his crew cab pickup—while juggling a wailing toddler in one arm and making frequent grabs for a wandering preschooler with the other. Poor guy. Women shouldn't send their helpless men out into the world without adequate kid training. And back up.

She sighed. She didn't have time for this tonight. Customers straggling in late with cross-country ski rental returns had delayed the closing of her mother's general store, Dix's Woodland Warehouse. Much longer and Mom would start wondering why she hadn't brought home the promised Friday night dinner from Kit's Lodge. A quick call would put her mind at ease, but being accountable to Mom again was already getting old. It was bitter cold, too, with wind whipping out of the northwest in buffeting gusts. No, it wasn't a good night to stop and offer a helping hand.

Nevertheless, she returned to the SUV she'd borrowed from her mom and retrieved a heavy-duty snowbrush. Then, securing her jacket's insulated hood, she approached the struggling male and raised her voice over that of the squalling child.

"Could you use some help?"

He swung toward her, his face in shadow.

She waved the snowbrush.

"Oh, man, thanks." His own raised voice held a note of grateful surprise as he endeavored to calm the unhappy little girl now flinging herself back and forth in his arms. "Didn't know it snowed so much while we were inside."

"That's mid-January in mountain country for you."

Before Kara could register what he was intending to do, the man stepped forward and thrust the flailing toddler at her. *What?* She didn't want to hold the kid. All she'd intended to do was help clean off the guy's truck. But the bundled-up, squalling tyke was stretching out arms to her. Even though she was irritated with "Daddy," Kara reluctantly relinquished the snowbrush and gathered the tiny screamer into her arms. Lovely.

The man snagged the sleeve of the older child and gently pushed her toward Kara as well, then turned to the truck and set to work. Through the passenger-side front window, she glimpsed a lop-eared, mixed-breed mutt taking in the outside activity with interest. Almost as if laughing at her.

Kara awkwardly jiggled the bawling little one and fished in her pockets—in vain—for a tissue to wipe the miniature nose. She winced as slobber-wet fingers brushed her face. Where was the kid's mitten? Kara glanced at the snow-covered ground but saw no sign of it, then caught the tiny, sticky hand in her own.

Hurry it up, Cowboy.

As she warmed the little hand, she caught the older child staring at her. Even in the dim light it was clear she didn't think this stranger was handling her sibling with any degree of expertise. Kara bestowed a weak smile. It was hard to tell through the dim light and pelting snow, but the face peeping out from under a hood looked familiar.

Kara made shushing sounds at the youngster in her

arms, then raised her voice over the howls. "What's your name?"

"Mary."

"Mary what?"

"Mary had a little lamb." The preschooler giggled and danced away.

Kara forced another smile. A comedian. She turned her attention again to the toddler who, for whatever mysterious reason, had abruptly quieted. Thank goodness. She'd pulled her tiny hand free, rubbed her nose and was now studiously exploring Kara's facial features with the tip of a moist finger. The girl giggled. Sniffled. Then hiccupped.

Kara turned her face aside to see what had happened to Cowboy. She shifted the kid and squinted through the steadily falling snow. Oh, there he was. On the far side of the pickup.

"Uh, you about done over there?"

"Almost. Hang on." He said something else but the wind snatched away the words.

Cowboy made a few more swipes with the brush, then limped around the front of the truck to open the passenger-side back door. He motioned to the older girl. "Hop in, Mary."

With a boost from him, the child obeyed. Then, tucking the snowbrush under his arm, he leaned inside the truck to harness her in a car seat.

"What's your phone number, sweetheart?" he called over his shoulder to Kara. "9-1-1-Kid-Help?"

He chuckled.

Her heart dipped. Then stilled.

She knew that laugh.

She shook her head, in part to loosen the tod-dler's fingers now snaking into the hair under her hood, but mainly to dash away the foolish imagining. Being back in Canyon Springs made her jumpy. Paranoid. And at the present moment, a little sick to her stomach.

It couldn't be *him*. No way. She'd have heard if he was back in town, wouldn't she? Then again, for the past six weeks she'd been buried alive managing the Warehouse for her mom. Taking on the household tasks and transporting her parent to out-of-town physical therapy appointments. There hadn't been a single moment to catch her breath, let alone catch up with in-the-know locals.

But maybe that's why the little girl looked familiar? He'd returned after all—had kids now? Her mind flashed back a dozen years to a tall, lean high school senior who'd moved to town her sophomore year. He'd had her female classmates swooning over a slow, lazy smile that she remembered well. T-shirt. Jeans. Western boots. Attitude.

But although she'd lain awake far too many nights dreaming about him, she'd steered clear. Mostly anyway. After all, he was a cowboy. Just like her no-good dad. That "troublemaking preacher's kid" the townspeople had labeled him.

Thanks mainly to her...

Please, God, don't let it be him.

"Ouch!" Cringing, she grabbed her earlobe and pried away tiny fingers. "Not the earring, kid."

The child pulled back and frowned, studying her a long moment. Big dark eyes. Another hiccup. Then the tiny face crumpled and the wailing began again.

Kara stepped to the open truck door. "Okay, Daddy, time to reclaim your kid."

"That's not Daddy," the older girl objected from the backseat, her tone indignant. "That's Uncle Trey."

Kara's breath caught.

The man backed out of the truck and turned to her, both of them now illuminated by the vehicle's interior light. Steady blue eyes met hers. In that flashing moment his gaze reflected the surprise of mutual recognition. A recognition that rocked her to the core, all but knocking the wind right out of her.

He'd changed. Filled out. Matured. Laugh lines crinkled at the corners of his eyes. The crooked nose he'd broken from a fall off a horse still imparted a rugged, reckless air to his countenance. Same strong jaw, now in need of a shave. Every bit as handsome as he'd ever been. And then some.

"Kara?"

Her gaze riveted, struggling for breath, she could only nod. He didn't try to jog her memory as to who he was. He knew she'd remember. He'd have read it in her eyes.

Oh, yes, she remembered Trey Kenton.

After a too-long moment, he gave a wry chuckle. "Didn't figure I'd ever run into you again."

She swallowed and held out the now-whimpering child. "I don't imagine you did."

He accepted his niece and handed over the snow-brush, but his eyes searched Kara's. For what? Confirmation that she was sufficiently ashamed of the cowardly lurch she'd left him in those many years ago?

Oh, yes, she remembered. Would never forget. Or forgive herself. So why should he?

She broke eye contact and motioned to the child fussing in his arms. "She lost her mitten."

How lame. She owed him an apology, not an evasive, impersonal observation.

He dug out a handkerchief and wiped the sniffling toddler's nose, then enveloped the tiny bare hand in his large gloved one. "She hasn't had a nap in days and now we're all paying for it."

Could he be as uncomfortable as she was? After all, the last time they saw each other… Her cheeks warmed at the memory.

"Come on, Uncle Trey. Let's go home."

"Hang on, Mary."

He focused again on Kara with a look she could only interpret as wary. Couldn't blame him.

"So, Kara, you're back in Canyon Springs."

She tightened her grip on the snowbrush. "Not for long. Helping my mom get back on her feet. She hasn't been well."

"Heard about that. Sorry."

Was he? Sharon Dixon and Trey Kenton hadn't

exactly been a match made in heaven. Cowboy types didn't easily endear themselves to her mom. Or her.

The wind kicked up again, swirling a stinging mix of snow and ice pellets into their faces.

"Need to get these kids home and tucked into bed." He turned to the truck and eased the toddler into the empty car seat next to that of her sister.

Kara stepped away on unsteady legs. Was he visiting? Just babysitting for his brother and sister-in-law? Surely he hadn't moved back to Canyon Springs. No way. From the moment he'd set a booted foot inside the city limits as a teen, he'd been determined to put the mountain community in his rearview mirror.

With speed that likely rivaled his best record at roping and tying a calf, Trey buckled in his niece. Then he shut the back door and turned to Kara once more, his face again shadowed. "Thank you kindly for your help."

With a brisk nod and a tip of his hat, he limped around the front of the truck to the driver's side and climbed in.

He didn't have a limp in high school.

Heart pounding in an erratic rhythm, she could only stare stupefied at the pickup as another gust of wind slammed into her. She hardly felt the cold creeping in around the neckline of her jacket or the wind-driven snowflakes pelting her face.

That was it? A coolly polite "thank you kindly for your help"? She took another step back, absently glancing down at the frosty ground—and spied a pint-size mitten lying half-buried in the snow. She knelt to pick it up with a trembling hand.

But before she could return it to its diminutive owner, the truck started—and the man whose life she'd all but ruined drove away.

Whoa. Trey gave a low whistle as he and the girls headed out of town to his brother and sister-in-law's place, the windshield wipers battling the pummeling snow.

Kara Dixon. Hadn't bargained on that one tonight.

He'd been in and out of Canyon Springs the past several months and knew she'd returned at Thanksgiving. Heard she was an interior designer with some big firm in Chicago. Had even glimpsed her a few times, helping her mother out of a car at the grocery store. Unloading boxes at the Warehouse. Dashing coatless across the street to Camilla's Café.

He'd intentionally kept his distance—even stayed away from town most weekends—but she wasn't a woman who'd be easily overlooked. Not with that toned figure and long, red-blonde mane of hers caught up in a ponytail. Strawberry blonde. That's how his sister-in-law described it. And Kara was model-tall and leggy, too, like a thoroughbred. He'd forgotten how it initially amused his seventeen-year-old self that ill-fated night when, in a sassy show of bravado, she'd walked right up to him, all but able to look him straight in the eye.

Just like her old man did to him now.

Well, maybe not *just* like. Her father's blustery shot at intimidation didn't send his heart galloping off like a wild mustang or his brain hurtling into a bottomless, fog-filled canyon. Didn't make his mouth go as dry as the Sonoran desert before summer monsoons kicked in.

Trey took a deep breath, still reliving the shock of turning to face her. No, he hadn't bargained on running into Kara up close and personal. And he sure hadn't bargained on feeling as if he'd collided with rock-hard Mother Earth, compliments of an irritable bronc. Even after all this time, even after what she'd done to him, he couldn't shake the impact of those beautiful gray eyes.

He let out a gust of pent-up breath. What was wrong with him anyway? He wasn't a kid anymore with a crush on the prettiest girl he'd ever seen—yet his heart was doing a too-familiar do-si-do, the rhythm beckoning him back through time.

He slammed the heel of his hand into the rim of the steering wheel, startling his dog, Rowdy, who rode shotgun on the seat next to him. He gave the Gordon setter-collie mix a reassuring pat and a feathered tail wagged in understanding.

Kara. No way was he going down that road again. He'd come back to town to lay the past to rest, not resurrect it. Thank the good Lord it sounded like she didn't plan to linger much longer. Just popping in to check on her mom. He needed to stay focused on the business at hand. Business, in fact, that Li'l Ms. Dixon wasn't going to be much pleased about once word got around. Which it eventually would in a tiny place like this.

In spite of himself, his mind's eye drifted to that long-ago night that now once again seemed like yesterday. The look in her eyes. The sweet scent of her hair. How she felt in his arms...

"Uncle Trey, why did you drive past our road?"

The accusing voice of his older niece carried from the shadowed recesses of the backseat, jerking him into the here and now.

"Just takin' the scenic route." He glanced into the rearview mirror at Mary, all the while racking his memory as to how much farther he'd have to drive to turn around with the empty trailer hitched to the back.

Kara Dixon was already messing with his mind.

"It's dark." Mary's petulant voice came again. "I want to go home."

She sounded as tired as he was. Three days playing both Mom and Dad had just about done him in. One more day to go.

"Your wish is my command, princess."

"I'm your princess?"

"You know it."

He glanced again at Mary, then over his shoulder at Missy and smiled. Sound asleep. He'd drive all night if it would keep her snoozing. What a day. He shouldn't have dragged them all the way to Holbrook this afternoon to look at that pony.

Seemed like a good idea at the time, but that was before a stronger cold front plowed into the region. Before he'd discovered the advertised pinto was an ill-tempered beast, certainly nothing he'd want his nieces having anything to do with. Then there had been the diaper dealings. A lesson learned the hard way. No, not a day he cared to relive anytime soon. His sister-in-law would laugh her head off.

It was just as well, though, that the trip was a bust. His brother would have killed him if he'd bought the girls a pony. With the parsonage remodel in town coming along on schedule, Jason and his wife wouldn't be staying at the cabin and acreage out in the boonies much longer. Which meant, too, he needed to give serious thought about what to do with himself. There wouldn't be any space at the parsonage for a tagalong brother.

At least he'd soon be able to move his horses to the equine center he and a group of investors were renovating. Last week his working-from-home office assistant had submitted the final documents for a permit to board his horses, so at least he didn't have to worry about that. Just needed to find office space until the facility's remodel was completed—and a place to throw down his bedroll until a house caught his fancy.

A couple of miles farther on, he pulled into the snowy, graveled lot of a long-abandoned bait and tackle shop. He got himself turned around and headed back in the right direction.

"What was that lady's name, Uncle Trey?" Mary piped up again.

"What lady is that? The pony woman?"

"No. The pretty one. Who was holding Missy."

He tightened his grip on the steering wheel. "Her name's Kara Dixon. We went to high school together."

"Did you kiss her?"

Memory flashed with an accompanying kick to his gut. Yes, he'd kissed her. Once. And fool that he was, a million other times in his dreams.

"Mommy said Daddy kissed *her* in high school when they were sixteen—on Valemtime's Day—and then they got married."

He smiled at her mispronunciation of the holiday.

"How old are you, Uncle Trey?"

"You're awfully full of questions tonight, squirt."

"Mommy says you need to kiss a girl and get married so you'll stay in Canyon Springs."

"Your mommy—" He stopped himself. Nothin' he'd like better than to settle down close to "his girls." That was the plan, but he didn't want to set Mary up for disappointment if it didn't work out. No point either in attempting to enlighten a four-year-old on his thoughts regarding the relentless mission of his sister-in-law. Except for the one date he'd managed to pull off behind her back, he'd steered clear of Reyna's matchmaking, and females in general, since his return to town.

He didn't need her hounding him about Kara Dixon. *Nosiree.* He wanted no part of the grown-up version of the girl from his past. The gray-eyed gal with a kissable mouth—who'd left him sittin' high and dry when the cops showed up.

Chapter Two

"Where'd you get this darling little thing, doll?"

"What?" Jerked from her Trey-troubled thoughts, Kara looked up from the breakfast table. Her mother, Sharon Dixon, stood in the kitchen doorway waving the Kenton girl's pink mitten.

She must have dropped it when she'd hung her coat on the enclosed back porch last night. Or had Mom been rifling through her pockets for cigarettes or other incriminating evidence of misbehavior, just as she'd once caught her doing when Kara was a teen? She cringed inwardly at the memory, thankful that even though their relationship wasn't always warm and fuzzy, they'd come a long way in the past decade. Or so she'd thought.

"Found it last night. Belongs to one of Pastor Kenton's kids, so I'll need to return it." No need to divulge how she knew who it belonged to. Hopefully Mom wouldn't ask.

"I may see Reyna this morning. If she's back from

the retreat." Her mother spoke in the raspy fragments of a former heavy smoker. "Ladies' tea at the church. I'll take it to her."

Over and over throughout the night Kara had waded through possible scenarios of returning it. Of using the opportunity to ask Trey's forgiveness. But of course her mom could return the mitten. That made the most sense. She couldn't face the child's uncle again anyway. How could she apologize without telling him the truth? A truth that she wasn't free to tell?

What am I going to do, God?

Her grip tightened on the fork in her hand. Why couldn't stupid choices made in the past be left *in* the past? And why did she keep wasting her breath, crying out to the Heavens about it? Hadn't she learned when Dad walked out that God had more important things to deal with than her?

Aware that Mom was watching with a curious tilt to her head, she set her fork on the stoneware plate and glanced out the paned windows of the cozy cinnamon-scented kitchen. A frosty blanket coated the towering ponderosa pines, lending the trees a holiday-ish flocked appearance. But she wasn't in a holiday mood. A blustering gust shook the powderlike crystals loose, flinging them into the air and sending a fairy dust cascade earthward. Sleet pecked on the window above the sink.

She shivered. Why'd Mom always keep it so cold in the house? "Is someone picking you up for the church thing, Mom, or do you want me to drive you? I don't want you walking in this. That wind's nasty."

"Peggy's coming by. You should come with us." Her mom brushed a hand through her layered auburn hair. "Lindi's giving a talk on community service. I think it's one of those 'it's not what Canyon Springs can do for you, but what you can do for Canyon Springs' spins. I know she'd love to see you."

Since returning to town she hadn't heard a peep out of her once-upon-a-time friend and cousin, Lindi Bruce. Did she know Trey was back?

"Unfortunately, there's nobody to cover for me." She folded her napkin and placed it on the worn wooden table by her plate. "Meg's visiting a hospitalized friend in Phoenix and won't be back until this afternoon. Roxanne has out-of-town company and asked for the day off."

"Then give Lindi a call next week. You haven't had a chance to catch up with any of your friends. Been too busy taking care of your feeble old mom."

"That's what I'm here for, Feeble Old Mom," she teased, then drained the last of her orange juice. "In case you've forgotten, if I wasn't helping you I wouldn't even be in town."

Her mother's lips tightened and Kara's heart sank. She'd said the wrong thing again. If only she could get along with Mom as well as her friend, Meg McGuire, got along with her. Every time she saw them together, laughing and on the same wavelength, jealousy stabbed. But then, Meg was everybody's sweetheart.

"Nevertheless," her mother continued, "with Lindi running for city council, you have lots of catching up to do. She's a dream candidate, even as young as she is—sure to give Jake Talford a run for his money. Her granddad's about to pop his buttons. You two girls make your families proud."

That was debatable.

She stood, then carried her plate and glass to the sink where she rinsed them off. The only time Mom was proud of her was when she was doing exactly what Mom wanted her to do. Like coming back to Canyon Springs.

She glanced at her watch. Seven-thirty. "Guess I'd better brush my teeth and head over to the Warehouse. With fresh snow, the more adventuresome types may look for outdoor activities. Maybe ski rentals will do a good business today."

"We can hope. The recession's lingering effects have hit the high country hard."

Kara frowned. Her mother and an accountant in Show Low looked after the books for Dix's Woodland Warehouse. Kara didn't have a clue about anything on the business side of her mother's store. "We're doing okay, though, aren't we? I mean, turning an adequate profit, right?"

Mom smiled. "Tightening the belt a bit. But don't go worrying about that."

"Well, you don't need to be worrying about stuff

like that either. Did you sleep okay last night? You look tired."

While her mom had only turned fifty-six last month, she'd gradually put on excessive pounds through the years. Which led to borderline diabetes and knee damage, and put her on a walker on bad days. But she'd lost considerable weight in the aftermath of her November heart attack and no longer had the round, merry face all had grown accustomed to. When Kara returned at Thanksgiving, it had been like coming home to a ghost of her mother.

Which scared her.

"I'm fine, doll."

"You have to be honest with me, Mom." She folded her arms in an attempt to feel in control, when all she wanted was to slip into the comfort of her mother's arms like she'd done when she was a little kid. Everything coming all at once—Mom's illness, taking leave from her job, Trey's return... It was too much. "If you're not feeling well, we need to get you checked out before things get out of hand again."

"I'm fine. Goodness knows you're not letting me do anything around here." Her mom chuckled. "Between both you and Meg helping, I've plumb become a lady of leisure."

"Take it easy today, okay? Get some rest. Going to that tea isn't a priority."

"Does me good to see everybody. Laugh a little."

She fixed a glare of mock reprimand on her parent. "Catch up on gossip?"

"Mercy me, at a church event?"

Laughing with Mom felt good. Why couldn't it be like this between them all the time?

"Speaking of gossip—" She paused, preparing to ask if her mom was aware that Trey Kenton had returned to town. Then she thought better of it. Should her mother confess, it would only lead to an argument. "Never mind."

If God had the time and inclination to take mercy on her, she'd be out of town in a couple of weeks and never have to see Trey again.

Trey kept his voice low as he spoke into his cell phone.

"Sure wish you'd stop talking about my love life in front of the girls, Reyna."

His sister-in-law's whoop echoed in his ear. "And what love life would that be?"

He pictured the wide smile of his brother's pretty, plump wife. White teeth flashing in contrast to her creamy Hispanic skin tone, her dark eyes dancing. Not only lovely, but her husband's number one fan, a great mom and a woman of deep faith. How'd his little brother rate such a catch? Must have extra pull in the heavenly realms.

"Very funny, Rey. But I'm serious."

"Ooh, serious, huh?" She giggled. "As in you're going to do what if I don't stop?"

"If you want me to stay here like you keep saying

you do, knock it off. Mary's too young to be fixating on kissing and romance and marriage and stuff."

"Kissing and stuff?" Reyna giggled again. "Were you dealing with birds and bees issues this week, Uncle Trey?"

Fighting a smile, he walked sock-footed across the cabin's hardwood floor to the living room, then pulled back one of the insulated drapes. Still snowing. "Put Jason on, will you?"

His sis-in-law laughed again, then he could tell she'd covered the mouthpiece to bring his younger sibling up to speed. They were in Tucson for a pastoral retreat, enjoying cactus and warm sunshine. Lucky dogs.

"Yo, bro." The voice of Jason Kenton, pastor of Canyon Springs Christian Church, greeted him. "Reyna giving you a hard time?"

Trey's smile broadened as he continued to stare at the wind-shaken ponderosa pines. "Is there ever a time she doesn't?"

"So, what's up?"

"Just checking in. You still planning to get home tonight?"

"Last session's over around noon. Hope to be home before dark." Jason paused. "But we're willing to stay another night if you'll cover the worship service tomorrow morning. And devotions at the care facility in the afternoon."

"Dream on, preacher man." His brother had been on his case for months to take a more active role in the family "business." "Unless, of course, you think your congregation can ferret out a deeper meaning in a ridin' and ropin' demonstration."

Jason chuckled, and Trey envisioned him scrubbing a hand alongside his neatly clipped beard, facial hair he'd grown in recent months in hopes of looking more mature.

"So, the girls behaving themselves this morning?"

"Still in bed." Trey raked a hand through his sleep-matted hair. "Hey, while I have you on the line—I was wondering if you remember the name of a guy who was in your graduating class. The one with the big ears and funny laugh. Couldn't even wait to get off school property before he'd pull out a cigarette and light up. Was always wanting to borrow my lighter."

"Pete. Pete Burlene." Jason paused for a moment. "Why? You think he's the one?"

"Grasping at straws is more like it."

"You know, Trey—" His younger brother let out a huff of air, then continued in his best pastoral tone that for some reason always irritated Trey. Even after four years in ministry in Canyon Springs, it remained a stretch for Jason to sound older and wiser than his twenty-eight years. "You have to ask yourself, bro, is it worth it? Worth getting tied up in knots trying to uncover the real culprit's identity?"

"Look, Jason—"

"If this is what it's going to do to you, maybe settling back in Canyon Springs isn't the best move after all." He lowered his voice. "In spite of what my wife thinks."

Trey's jaw tightened. Jason still didn't get it. "I don't think there's any harm in trying to clear my name."

"But look what it's doing to you. And you're no closer to finding out who left your lighter at the scene of that fire than when you first hit town. Face it. It's been twelve years."

"Every man needs a hobby."

Jason scoffed.

"Look, Jas, injury cost me my livelihood. Then my new job brings me back here. You're the one who's always saying there's no such thing as coincidence. Doesn't it sound to you like God's providing an opportunity for resolution? Justice?"

"'Fraid I can't speak for the Man Upstairs on this one, dude."

What he meant was he thought his big brother was chasing after something better left alone. Well, he could think whatever he wanted. He wasn't the one locals looked at with suspicion. Nobody questioned his honesty. His integrity. They didn't whisper behind *his* back.

"It's a shame," Jason continued, "that you were such a loner—and that our folks had taken me to Phoenix to catch a plane for that spring break mission trip. You didn't have anyone to confirm you were nowhere near Duffy's place when the property caught fire."

Trey's lips tightened. It didn't do you any good to

have a rock-solid alibi if your star witness refused to come forward.

"Well, Jas, I'll let you get back to your retreat. I have to pick up my toys, then hit the shower before the girls wake up." He glanced around at the cabin strewn with kid stuff. A diaper bag toppled on its side. Stuffed animals and dolls in various stages of dress piled on the sofa. Pint-size shoes and socks under the coffee table. Yesterday's dishes still in the sink. How'd it get to be such a disaster in only three days?

Jason barked a laugh. "Why do I have a feeling the girls will have lots to tell us when we get home?"

Trey groaned. "Yeah, well, just remember you owe me one."

"You got it, buddy."

"Take it easy coming up the mountain. Snowing."

"Will do."

Trey shut off the phone and again stared out the window at the swirling, wind-whipped flakes, making no move to wrestle his surroundings to order.

He shook his head as memories he'd fought all night resurfaced. Kara Lee Dixon. If he wasn't mistaken, she'd been as surprised to see him last night as he'd been to see her. Maybe more so. Hadn't she known he was back in town? Not from the look on her face. The fear in her expressive eyes.

What did she think he'd do after all these years? Chew her out on a public street? Make a spectacle of himself in front of the girls? Call the cops? No, he'd long ago forgiven her.

He hadn't handled their reunion well. Caught off guard, he'd been every bit as tongue-tied around her as he'd ever been as a teen. Practically threw Missy in the truck, then climbed in and hit the gas. That must have impressed the former girl of his dreams.

But like it or not, he and Kara needed to have a little chat.

Chapter Three

"I can't believe you didn't tell me you went out with Trey Kenton last fall." Kara looked up from where she knelt mopping a front corner of the Warehouse floor and leveled a disbelieving stare at her old college roommate.

Meg McGuire, soon to be Mrs. Joseph Diaz, had stopped by mid-afternoon Saturday to collect a trunk full of flattened cardboard boxes. Now here she stood, handing Kara another old bath towel and delivering the dismaying confirmation that Trey was indeed considering moving back to town. He was heading up a renovation of Duffy Logan's old horse facility, a property that had closed and fallen into disrepair almost a decade ago when Duffy suffered a debilitating stroke and his wife moved him out of town for better medical care. But why would Trey come back here of all places? Right smack-dab on top of the scene of the crime that drove him from town as a teenager?

"How would I know you had any connection to Trey?" Meg's eyes narrowed with interest beneath the fluffy bangs of her short, brunette hair. "When your name came up one time, I couldn't tell if he even remembered you."

Oh, he remembered her all right.

"He definitely recalled that old car of yours," Meg continued with a teasing tone.

Kara's memory flashed to the infamous '63 Mustang. The sporty, cream-colored car her daddy had lovingly restored and left behind when he took off for new adventures. He'd had the gall to transfer the registration to her as a sweet sixteen birthday gift. It still sat in the garage behind her mother's house.

"I sense a story here." Meg's eyes sparkled with a speculative gleam. "Were you and Trey sweeties? Hmm?"

Warmth crept into Kara's cheeks as she wiped the wooden floor with a fresh towel, then got to her feet. She'd told her mom about the leak last spring, yet the trickle again coursed down the wall from ceiling to floor. From the looks of the warped plaster and paint discoloration above, the summer monsoon season had added to the damage. Now the snow. So much for the expertise of repairmen.

"Trey and I were friends. Sort of." How could she explain the mixed-up adolescent relationship she didn't even understand herself?

"Friends, huh? Your mom mentioned you had a

crush on my Joe once upon a time, but she never mentioned Trey."

Kara laughed. "Mom talks too much."

She crossed the rustic, wood-beamed room to spread soppy bath towels on the bricked portion of the floor in front of the woodstove. "Joe was my crush of the moment in middle school—when I found out his mom walked out on him like my dad did me. Besides, there wasn't anything to mention about Trey—except Mom didn't like him."

She lifted an insulated carafe from its perch next to the coffeemaker and poured a mug of spiced cider for Meg. She'd kept her more-than-friends feelings for Trey a secret from the world those many years ago. Seemed strange to be openly teased about him now. And why did her heart tap-dance at the mere mention of his name, just like it had at sixteen?

"She didn't like him because of the cowboy connection? Because of your dad?" Meg cupped the mug in her hands and inhaled the fragrant brew. "Or because, you know, of that other thing?"

Kara stiffened, the carafe poised above another mug. "You've heard about that?"

Meg nodded, her expression curious.

"Mom always said cowboys were trouble." Kara filled the second mug to the brim. "But he didn't do it. So don't believe anything you hear to the contrary."

"I didn't learn about it until after I went out with him. But I wasn't about to believe it. I'm glad my instincts were on target." She took a sip of cider. "So, then, if you weren't sweethearts, why are you all bent out of shape that he could be moving back to town?"

"I'm not bent out of shape." Kara met her friend's gaze, doing her best to keep her voice from betraying the turmoil inside. Meg wasn't trying to be nosy. They'd been open with each other in college, sharing all the secrets young women held dear. Except the one having to do with Trey. "I'm surprised, that's all. Didn't expect to run into him last night. You might find this hard to believe, as enamored as you are with Canyon Springs, but he hated this town."

"He's never mentioned that to me."

"You've talked a lot?"

"Some."

Was Meg being deliberately obtuse, trying to draw her out? To get her to say more than she had any intention of saying?

"He's so sweet," her friend rambled on, a playful twinkle in her eye. "And single. Never married."

"If he's such a great catch," Kara fired back with a grin, "why aren't you marrying him instead of Joe?"

She couldn't picture Meg and Trey as a good match, but nevertheless a fleeting tingle of envy pierced her consciousness. After all, Meg had dated him not long ago. What had that been like? Trey, all grown up. A man.

"I was falling for Joe by the time I met Trey." Meg's

eyes went dreamy, so at least she hadn't been forced to come to a heartrending decision between the two men.

"Just remember, Meg—" she took a sip of cider before setting down the mug "—if you want to make it to your wedding day alive, don't even think of trying to set me up with him."

"Vannie Quintero, the teen who works at my future father-in-law's campground, is thrilled to be teamed up with an ex-cowboy." Meg winked. "Maybe you would be, too."

"Don't count on it." Kara gave in to a smile and tossed her ponytail over her shoulder. She'd hardly believed it when Meg had told her Trey agreed to mentor a high school kid. Or that no one, considering his own teenage track record, voiced objections. "Besides, there's no such thing as an *ex*-cowboy."

"You never can tell. With the right woman…" Meg gave her a mischievous poke in the arm. "Now that I'm going to be more than a temporary resident of Canyon Springs, I wish you'd move back, too. Think of all the fun we'd have."

"Fun?" she countered with a grin of her own. "Like watching you and Joe cuddling up on the sofa, eyes glued to each other like at the New Year's Eve party a couple of weekends ago?"

"Hook up with Trey," Meg said, wiggling her eyebrows, "then go thou and do likewise."

Kara shook a finger at her. "I'm warning you—"

Her friend had all but bubbled with happiness since

she and Joe got engaged. Must be nice. Not that she resented her friend's good fortune to find a guy like the ex-navy corpsman with a cute kid. Meg more than deserved a happily ever after. But if Kara had the misfortune to return permanently, she'd likely seldom see her old friend. With Meg's full-time teaching job, a soon-to-be husband, new stepson—and probably future kids—that didn't leave much time to hang out.

Besides, Canyon Springs wasn't in her future. Never had been. Never would be.

She held up her hand, thumb and forefinger pressed together. "I'm *this* far from that promotion. And I'm sure my supervisor wouldn't appreciate my ditching him right now. Not after he's gone out of his way to cover for me while I'm checking in on Mom. I promised to be back in two more weeks, and I take my promises seriously."

Her memory flickered to the last conversation she'd had with her supervisor and mentor, Spencer Alexander. He'd laughed, but not in a derogatory way, when she'd let it slip that her father had been a rodeo cowboy. He'd called her his "little cowgirl."

"And don't forget," she continued. "I came back here for a few weeks last spring when that new medication got Mom's system all out of whack. And when she fell last summer. Unpaid time off isn't helping my professional reputation—or my savings account. I'm still covering my quarter of the rent and utilities on the apartment even when I'm not there. Making car payments, too."

Meg gave an exaggerated sigh. "I'm thrilled you're getting a chance to live your dream. But I can dream, too, can't I?"

"Dream away. But don't hold your breath."

Meg glanced at her watch, then set her mug down before snatching her jacket off the back of a nearby chair. "Thanks for helping me load the boxes. I'd better get going. Have a few things to finish up before we start carting things over to the new place tonight. Joe's dad let us store my Phoenix furniture at the RV park's rec center until we got the house livable."

With another twinge of unexpected envy, Kara recalled the cute little place Meg and Joe bought last month and where Meg would now be living prior to the wedding. She'd helped her spruce up the kitchen last week. A little paint and a lot of elbow grease. New floor tile laid and curtains hung.

"You're still having a move-in party tonight? Even with the snow?"

"Yeah. It'll be messy, which is why I want to cut up boxes to protect the hardwood floor." Meg zipped her coat and dug gloves out of her pockets. "Joe starts official paramedic training Monday and he wants me settled in before he leaves."

Kara motioned to the ceiling. "Even though you weren't in the upstairs apartment for long, I'm going to miss you."

"I'll miss you, too. It was great not to have to spend

the past six weeks in the RV. Your mom wouldn't even take rent money—said to consider it an engagement gift. Can you believe it? But I'm sure she could use a paying tenant."

"She wouldn't have offered it if she'd needed the money."

Meg's smile widened. "Now I have a wedding to finish planning, don't I? Spring break will be here before we know it. Speaking of which, Joe's Aunt Rosa started sewing your maid of honor dress. Hopefully she'll be far enough along for a final fitting before you leave."

Bells above the store's front door tinkled, sounding merrier than Kara felt, and the pair glanced at a bundled-up couple entering the welcoming warmth of the general store.

"Looks like I'd better let you get back to work." Meg stepped forward to give her a hug. "Good luck on getting the leak fixed. See you tonight?"

Kara nodded, but it was with a heavy heart that she watched her friend out the door. Even though Meg didn't seem to sense it, she didn't like the invisible wall that reared itself between them with Trey's return. But there was no way she'd attempt to explain to her what she'd done to him. Meg was so enthralled with Trey, she'd never understand. She'd certainly think far less of her college friend if she knew.

Already dreading an evening where Trey might show up, Kara grabbed a dust cloth and gave the checkout counter a swipe, then paused to gaze around the familiar expanse of the Warehouse. The paned windows. Plank floors. Well-stocked grocery items and other general merchandise. Displays of mountain country souvenirs and outdoor gear.

The knot in her stomach tightened. Why hadn't her cousin Lindi alerted her to Trey's return? Lindi. The reason she couldn't tell Trey the truth. Beg his forgiveness. It was twelve years ago this very spring that her confused and scared, barely sixteen-year-old self had made the promise. Pledged that she wouldn't tell a soul her best-friends-forever cousin had confessed to accidentally setting the forest on fire.

By the time she'd found out Trey had been accused…it was too late. She'd already made that impulsive vow that still reached out to haunt her. Just one more sign that while God may have set her world in motion, kept it spinning, he was most often off in another sector of the universe.

"Hey, Trey!" Meg grabbed his snow-covered, jacketed arm, hauling him and his nieces off the porch and into the house she and Joe would soon be calling home. "You're just in time for pizza."

He stepped onto the rug by the door, Missy in his arms and Mary clinging shyly to his leg. He gazed around a room full of people helping themselves to the savory, mouthwatering contents of cardboard delivery boxes. He glimpsed a few familiar faces— Meg's fiancé and his dad and son. A dozen or two others he guessed to be church friends or teacher pals of Meg. Some of Joe's buds.

Recognition flickered in the gazes of several guests. That was to be expected in a small town. Warm interest reflected in the smiles of a few of the younger women. That was usually to be expected as well—wherever.

But no Kara.

Thank you, Lord.

He almost hadn't come, thinking she might be here, that it might be awkward, but he hated to back out on Meg. The perky newcomer to town had held a special place in his heart ever since they met last September. If it wasn't for that hotshot Diaz guy, it might be him settling down with the pretty schoolteacher. Or at least that's what he told himself on poor-pitiful-me days. But by the time he'd gotten her to go out with him, she was already falling for the ex-navy guy, one of Reyna's cousins. Meg hadn't realized it yet, but Trey had, and he backed off.

"Sorry I'm late, Meg. I've been babysitting the past few days and Jason and Reyna still aren't home yet."

A chorus of soft *aahs* echoed from female throats and inwardly he chuckled. It hadn't taken long to figure out that if you wanted to score interest with the local ladies, babysitting by far outweighed the classic walking-the-pup routine.

"Yeah, yeah," Joe's father, Bill Diaz, taunted, his

mustached mouth widening in a smile. "Timed it just right so all the heavy lifting's done."

"Guess you cowboys aren't as dumb as you look." The dark-eyed Joe cast him an appraising glance, a look he'd become accustomed to during the months Joe'd been courting Meg and keeping an eye open for rivals.

Relax, dude. She's all yours now.

"Don't listen to them, Trey," Meg said as he toed off his boots at the door. "You can make yourself useful bringing in the sodas—which my loving fiancé forgot to do."

A slice of pizza halfway to his mouth, Joe made sounds of protest.

"Consider it done." Trey would rather do something constructive than stand around making small talk with people he didn't know. People who may have formed judgments about him based on rumor. Coming back to Canyon Springs held more than its share of challenges. But God opened doors and he was gonna be man enough to walk through them no matter what it took.

Meg reached out for Missy, then he knelt to divest Mary of her coat. He peeled out of his own jacket and tossed their stuff on a folding table piled high with outdoor wear. Not trusting the guests to know a genuine Stetson when they saw one, he hesitated to top off the mound with his felt hat. But his ever-alert hostess snatched it from him and slid it onto a peg by the front door, then pointed in the direction of the kitchen.

With Mary gripping the welted side seam of his jeans, he made his way through the crowd, following the cardboard carpet past the staircase and into the kitchen. Looked like new floor tile. Fresh paint job on the cabinets, too. Curtains at the windows. Nice. Meg's doing? Or Kara's?

He'd have to figure out something homey like that when he bought a fixer-upper of his own. Having scrimped and saved every spare dime of his rodeo winnings for a hefty down payment, he had his heart set on a little house, some acreage. Had been looking forward for years to a day when he could settle down, start a family. A place like this, on the edge or outside of town, would be ideal. That is, if he cleared his name and made a go of the business. Old Reuben Falkner, city councilman, wasn't making the latter an easy effort.

He headed to an open door where Meg had indicated he'd find the laundry room. A light was on, but when he stepped to the doorway of the miniscule room, he halted. A familiar red-blonde ponytail dangled halfway down the back of a trim female dressed in figure-skimming jeans and a blue wool sweater.

Kara.

With her back to him, she wiped off soda cans arranged on the clothes dryer's surface. He had a second to catch his breath. But no time to back out the door before, head down and lost in thought, she whirled in his direction. Ran smack into his chest.

"Oh!" Her long-lashed gray eyes met his as she took a startled step back, pulling away from his hand that had instinctively reached out to steady her. For a long moment their gazes held. Every bit as close and as beautiful as she'd been that long-ago night. The night she'd sashayed up to him. Slipped her arms around his neck...

But tonight her eyes were that of a filly fixin' to bolt.

"I didn't hear you." Face flushing, she took another step back and glared at his socked feet as if he'd deliberately shed his boots to sneak up on her.

"Sorry. I was put on soda duty."

Kara frowned, apparently irritated Meg hadn't thought her capable to handle the task on her own. Then she spied Mary clutching his leg and her expression softened. She motioned to the cans.

"You can haul some of these to the living room if you'd like. Or break up that bag of ice in the chest there."

"Ice or sodas, doesn't matter to me." He chuckled, hoping to catch her eye and put her at ease, but she kept her focus on anything but him.

"Ice then."

He nodded and they did an uneasy tango as he and Mary maneuvered around her, the air charged with an unmistakable, mutual awareness. Had twelve years really gone by?

She took a sidestep toward the now-vacated doorway, but without thinking he shot out his arm to block her. Wary eyes met his. His breath caught at the light scent of her woodsy perfume.

"We need to talk, Kara."

Where'd that come from? He'd been hangin' out with his sister-in-law too long. Starting to sound like a girl. But all he needed was a lousy five minutes. He'd ditch Mary and make Kara understand he didn't hold anything against her. That she could stop looking at him like he was going to haul her into court.

Her brows lowered. "I—"

"Trey, did you bring Rowdy with you?" the familiar voice of five-year-old Davy Diaz called from across the kitchen.

Trey stared at Kara a long moment, his heartbeat counting off the seconds. Then he lowered his arm and turned to the youngster who trotted across the floor toward him and Mary. *Bad timing, kid.* But he'd sensed Kara's relief.

He gazed down at the black-haired, brown-eyed boy and smiled at the youngster's reference to his canine sidekick. Kids loved Rowdy. "We can't stay long, so he's out in the truck. That woolly coat of his keeps him toasty warm."

"Daddy wouldn't let me bring my puppy." Davy's shoulders slumped as he crammed his hands in his jeans pockets in an adultlike gesture. A miniature little man. His dark eyes brightened as he studied his cousin, Mary, who'd loosened a grip on Trey's pant leg and taken a hesitant step forward.

"Kara's already seed it," the boy continued, "but do you guys wanna see my new room? I'm gonna live here when we marry Miss Meg."

Mary looked up at Trey, hope in her eyes.

How could he turn down such cool kids? He glanced at Kara, but she again avoided his gaze. "I'd like to, Davy, but after I finish up here, okay? You two go on without me."

"No, go right ahead," the woman next to him insisted, all but shoving him out the door. "I can handle things here."

All I need, Lord, is five stinkin' minutes.

Granted, the other thing he needed to explain would likely take more than five minutes—if she'd hear him out at all. Her father had told him the two of them still weren't on speaking terms. Hadn't been for fifteen years. But he'd need to get her old man's permission to discuss it with her anyway.

He hauled Mary into his arms and Davy stepped forward to grab his free hand. Glancing back as the little boy pulled him along, he caught Kara's skittish gaze. Gave her a nod.

"We still need to talk, darlin'."

Chapter Four

We need to talk.

Ugh. Kara rummaged in a laundry room drawer until she found a small, metal mallet, then she knelt by the insulated chest to break up the bag of solidifying crushed ice. No wonder men hated that phrase when women accosted them with it.

So he thought they needed to talk? Until he walked into the room and she literally ran into him, she'd have agreed. She'd intended, at some point, to apologize as best she could. But not here. Not now. And certainly not after seeing the mutual memory of her immature teenage behavior spark in his expressive eyes. Heard his breath catch when their gazes held for a too-long moment. No, not the shared memory of his being abandoned to the law. Rather, an even more vivid memory of her boldly stepping up to him. Thoroughly kissing him. Making a suggestion she had no business making.

He'd rejected it on the spot.

She gave the ice another series of whacks that sent shattered fragments flying, then stood. She'd been young and stupid back then. Probably every bit as stupid even now because every fiber of her being cried out to dash into the cold, dark night as far from Trey as she could get.

She shouldn't have come this evening. She'd anticipated a few awkward, public moments if he showed up for Meg's party. Steeled herself for superficial greetings. Self-conscious small talk. But she hadn't anticipated him hunting her down, corralling her in the laundry room for one-on-one time. Wanting to settle old scores. Here. Tonight.

With shaky hands she dumped the contents of the plastic bag into the cooler with a resounding clatter.

"What's taking so long?" Meg appeared in the doorway of the laundry room, Trey's niece, the infamous screamer, in her arms. Thank goodness the contrary little thing seemed content enough tonight. Maybe her uncle had gotten her down for a nap.

"Where's Trey? I sent him to help you."

So much for warning her old friend not to matchmake.

"Davy dragged him upstairs to look at his room."

"Men." Meg made a silly face, then frowned. "You okay? You look kinda funny."

Hope sparked. Now was an ideal opportunity to make her getaway. "A little tired, I guess. Everything from the past weeks is catching up with me. Think

I'll cut out early. Get to bed at a decent hour for a change."

"You sure?"

She nodded, anxious to retrieve her coat and boots and get out of there. But she'd no more thought it than light footsteps followed by heavier ones clambered down the staircase. Glancing past Meg, she saw Davy and Mary head to the living room and a frowning Trey step into the kitchen, a finger poked in one ear and his cell phone pressed to the other.

He moved to the French doors leading to the patio, flipped on the exterior light and peered into the night. "You're kidding. Yeah, it's snowing harder up here, but—"

He turned as Meg and Kara entered the kitchen as well, then covered the mouthpiece. "Jason. DPS won't let anyone come up the mountain tonight."

"Oh, no," Meg whispered, giving Missy a hug.

But Missy paid her little attention, her wide dark eyes fixed on Kara, a dainty hand reaching toward her. Kara managed a weak smile in the child's direction, hoping Mighty Mouth wasn't fixing to treat them to a replay of last night's deafening rendition. She tossed her ponytail over her shoulder and cautiously eased away.

Trey continued to listen to his brother, his expression broadcasting dismay with the Arizona Department of Public Safety. He cleared his throat. "Sure, I can cover the care facility stuff. But come on, I don't know how to preach."

Kara and Meg exchanged a glance. Jason wanted Trey to preach tomorrow?

"No, no. Don't lose any sleep over it. I'll figure something out." He switched the phone to his other ear. "What? Naw. I don't think it's gonna get that bad."

He again glanced out the glass panes. Snow whipped out of the darkness, piling up at the base of the door. "Well, if it comes to that, maybe we can get a motel room. Don't want to impose on anybody. But I don't think—"

Meg and Kara exchanged puzzled glances.

"No, don't worry. I'll handle it. Yeah. Yeah. You, too."

He shut off the phone and let out a gusty sigh. Then he looked over at them, his smile tight. "He says if we get what DPS says we're going to get, there's no way I can dig out from his place in the morning in time to cover at the church."

Meg's face crinkled in sympathy. "They had to stay overnight with her folks a few weeks ago when we got that foot and a half of snow. I've been out there— that forest service road is super-primitive. So you're covering for Jason tomorrow?"

"Looks like it. He says it's too late to call a member of the congregation to fill in. Unfortunately," Trey continued with a glance in her direction, "Reyna's folks are out of town and I don't know her siblings well enough to show up on their doorsteps. So I guess we'd better get moving if I'm going to get the girls settled in at a motel."

He took Missy from Meg's arms, but the little girl's brown eyes remained fixed on Kara. "I'm totally unprepared except for a truckload of diapers, but that snow's accumulating fast."

"Oh, forget the motel, Trey. I'm sure Joe and his dad would put you up for the night." Meg motioned to the interior of her house. "The girls can stay with me. Plenty of room here for Rowdy, too."

"Thanks, but I couldn't—"

Meg cut him off with a snap of her fingers, her eyes brightening. "No, no, wait. I have a better idea. Kara and I have the perfect solution to your predicament."

"You do?" His voice held a note of wariness.

Kara didn't like the sound of her friend's proposal either. "We do?"

"Sure we do." Meg stepped across the kitchen, then pulled her purse from a lower cabinet shelf. A moment later she swung around, dangling a key from a fluorescent pink pom-pom key ring.

"Ta da! Remember the apartment I just vacated? Dix's Woodland Warehouse Bed-and-Breakfast to the rescue."

From the look on Kara's face an hour ago when Meg extended the unexpected invitation, he was in the doghouse for sure. Their mutual friend's enthusiastic offer had caught both of them off guard. He'd done his best to protest, to give Kara an out, but an oblivious Meg insisted it was the ideal solution. Caught in the middle, Kara had done the only thing she could do— echoed her old friend's generous suggestion. Assured him she was more than happy to put him and his nieces up at the Warehouse.

But he knew better.

Nevertheless, here he was in the second-floor apartment, ready to get the girls settled in. Meg kept Rowdy for the night, and Kara indicated she'd be by shortly to make sure they had everything they needed for the unplanned sleepover.

He watched his giggling nieces explore the unfamiliar space, looking none too sleepy if he was any judge. It was a church night, though, so he had to get them tucked in soon. Then he had to figure out a plan for tomorrow's worship service. And the visit to Pine Country Care.

But first things first.

When Kara showed up, they'd have that little talk he'd promised, even if he had to lasso the little lady to do it.

She'd throttle Meg later.

Lodging a complaint, insisting her friend withdraw the offer, would have made her seem petty. Tightening her grip on the overflowing fabric shopping bag, she exited by the Warehouse's front door and locked up. Then, scurrying through the deepening snow, she made her way toward a recessed door between the stone-fronted Warehouse and the adjacent bakery.

She didn't appreciate Meg's interference—especially after she'd asked her not to set her up with the cowboy. Even if they didn't have a canyon-size gulf from their past yawning between them, she and Trey didn't know each other anymore. Had never known each other. Not really. He'd moved to town in November of his senior year. The fire had been in late March, after a series of drought-ridden years. So five months max. Yet she'd spent over a decade bound to him. Chained by guilt.

Gathering her courage, she pulled open the glass-paned door and started up the steep, dimly lit stairs like a condemned prisoner heading for the guillotine. She'd do her best to drop off the bag and make a hasty exit. But what if he tried to corner her as he'd done at Meg's? Demand an explanation of her cowardice and a long overdue apology?

He had every right. She owed him that.

But not tonight.

At the sound of little girl giggles, running feet and Trey's cowboyish whoops coming from a door left ajar at the top of the stairs, she paused. The Trey she'd known in those few short months hadn't been criminally rebellious like some of their peers. No, he just went quietly about his business doing whatever he wanted to do, whether it was not completing homework, skipping school so he could spend more time with the horses at Duffy's or sneaking an occasional cigarette. In all honesty, it was her own cowardice that sealed his troublemaker image in the mind of the community. Now here he was a dozen years later, a guy with a toddler in his arms and another curtain climber hanging on his leg. A regular family man. No, they didn't know each other. At all.

At the top of the stairs it was tempting to leave the shopping bag looped over the doorknob and make her escape. But curiosity won over and she gave the door a push. Peeked inside as a giggling Missy, her chubby little legs pumping as fast as they could go, dodged Trey's outstretched hands.

The apartment's unobstructed, hardwood expanse made it much too appealing for an active toddler. In fact, except for the bathroom and kitchen, the nonstorage portion of the second floor consisted of a single room divided by a wide, bolted-down bookcase that separated the sleeping quarters from the front area. Perfect for an energetic little kid, as Kara remembered from her own childhood.

She stepped inside as Missy sped by.

"Don't just stand there laughing, woman, catch her!" Trey lunged again, sliding on the polished wooden floor in his socks. Then he righted himself and in a few quick steps swept the still-giggling toddler into his arms for a bear hug.

Kara couldn't help but clap her approval of the

child's antics—and Trey's agile performance. She should have known a cowboy, once he got the hang of it, could round up a kid as easily as a calf.

Still clutching the shopping bag, butterfly wings hammering against the wall of her stomach, she carefully wiped her boots on the rug by the door. "My mom said I did exactly the same thing in here when I was little."

A grinning Trey approached, Missy squirming in his arms. "You lived up here?"

"From birth through preschool. This was my folks' first place in Canyon Springs, right above their new business."

Trey assessed the space with a critical eye. "Now that Meg's moved out, does your mom have any plans for it?"

Uh-oh. That sounded like a more-than-casual query. She didn't want Trey upstairs. Didn't want him in Canyon Springs at all. Mustering a benign smile, she cut him off at the pass. "She'll need the extra storage space for inventory expansion. Besides, as you can probably tell, it's not that well insulated. Cold in the winter and hot in the summer."

The dark-eyed Missy stretched out a hand to her but she pretended not to notice.

"Meg didn't have any complaints." He glanced toward Mary who'd wandered to the far side of the room. He took a step closer to Kara and lowered his voice, apparently wanting to make sure the little girl was out of earshot. "Don't want to talk about this in front of Mary—"

She tensed. Was he going to call her on the carpet? Right here and now?

"—but I've already worn out my welcome at my little brother's place. They'll be moving back to the parsonage soon, so I need an office and a place to bunk. This would be just the ticket."

"Don't think Mom would go for that."

The slow smile that still made Kara's heart skip a beat surfaced. "Why not?"

She glanced at the boots standing at attention by the door. A hat nestled on a bookcase shelf, out of reach of the girls. Then looked him over. Worn jeans. Tooled leather belt with a silver buckle. Western-cut burgundy shirt unbuttoned at the collar. Just like in high school, only a more muscled, more grown-up version of the senior classmate she remembered.

"I don't think she'd go for, you know, a cowboy type."

"No cowboys, huh?" He pried Missy's fingers from his earlobe, but his amused gaze didn't leave Kara's face. "That's discrimination, Kara."

"What I mean is, if Mom was looking for a renter— which she's not—she'd be expecting a steady income. A stable tenant who'd stick around awhile."

"Then we're in business." He slapped his left leg, the apparent source of the limp. "Busted myself up so many times my surgeon's washed his hands of me. Says I'd better not get on another bronc or bull or I could end up in traction the rest of my life. I'm grounded for good. So I'm your man."

Her breath came a little quicker. Her man? Maybe in her dreams. Unfortunately, cowboying wasn't the only drawback to Trey Kenton. She might as well be blunt. "Mom will remember you as you were in high school."

"Boys grow up." A friendly but assessing gaze slid over her and a smile quirked again. "Girls do, too."

Their gazes met. How easy it would be to fall back into that old flirtatious teenage banter they used to share. The chemistry had stood the test of time, but she couldn't risk it.

"Well, since Mom's not looking to rent—"

"Maybe I'll give her a call."

He wouldn't, would he? She lifted the shopping bag still clutched in her hand and held it out to him. It was time to make her escape.

"I stopped off at the Warehouse and got you a few things. Breakfast cereal and a half gallon of milk. T-shirts for the girls to sleep in. Toothpaste. Toothbrushes. A comb. Razor."

Eyes twinkling, Trey caressed Missy's soft cheek with the back of his hand. "Noticed the girls need a shave, did you?"

"Right." Heart pounding, she handed off the bag and dragged her gaze from the firm jaw that once again showed evidence of a dusky shadow. "Snow's still dumping, so I need to get going. Bedding's in the chest over there. Meg said she'd washed it up. Washer and dryer behind the louvered doors." She glanced at him again, still avoiding Missy, who now leaned forward in his arms, hands outstretched toward her. "Do you need any help with anything?"

She hoped not. But as the hostess for his overnight stay, she had to at least offer.

"No, you've been more than generous." He set the bag on a nearby upholstered chair, the expression in his eyes becoming serious. Searching.

Oh, no. "Well, I'll see you later then. Sleep tight."

She turned toward the door, but he stepped forward to catch the upper arm of her coat sleeve.

Not now. I need to apologize. Beg his forgiveness. But not tonight. Not now.

He tugged on her sleeve and she momentarily closed her eyes, willing her heart to quiet. Even ventured a prayer. Then took a quick breath and faced him again.

He released her arm but held her gaze. "I know you need to get going, but I'm sorry Meg put you on the spot—offering the apartment without asking you first."

"Happy to help out." Happy? What a liar she was.

He glanced down at the floor, then back at her as if uncertain how to proceed. "Look, Kara, for whatever reason, we seem to have gotten off on the wrong foot at Meg's tonight. Maybe even last night in the parking lot at Kit's."

She clasped her still-gloved hands. "Guess we were both caught off guard."

He shifted Missy in his arms and thrust out a hand, his gaze penetrating hers. "What do you say then? Truce?"

Chapter Five

Now. Apologize now.

But she hesitated, her jaw tightening as their gazes held. She nibbled her lower lip, then took a ragged breath.

A truce.

"I guess it all depends." She lifted her trembling chin.

Trey withdrew his outstretched hand, his expression uncertain. "On what?"

She swallowed. *Now. Say it now.* "On if you can forgive me for not coming forward after the fire. For not—"

Trey held up a hand to halt her, then nodded to Mary who was now checking out the contents of Kara's shopping bag only a few feet away.

She'd totally forgotten about the little girl's presence.

"Honey—" he smiled at his niece "—why don't you trot on into the bathroom and get ready for bed?

Kara's got something in the bag for you to wear to sleep in. I'll be in to help you in a few minutes."

Moving to crouch down by the child and shopping bag, Kara pulled out an adult-size, pink *I Love Arizona* T-shirt. She'd hoped the girls would like the shimmery trim and the satin ribbon threaded along the hem, a delicate bow tied off to the side. Judging by the delight on Mary's face when she handed it to her, she'd guessed right.

Eyes wide, Mary glanced at her uncle, then smiled at Kara with that same slow smile Trey sported. "How old are you, Kara?"

"No, Mary." Trey shook his head at his niece. "Don't start with that again."

The preschooler giggled and clasped the T-shirt to her chest, her gaze intent as she took in Kara's hair, her face. Almost as if trying to memorize her every feature. "Thank you, Kara."

"You're welcome."

Then without warning the black-haired girl threw her arms around Kara for a hug. A tight one. Smelling of baby shampoo.

A warm whisper tickled Kara's ear. "I like you."

Kara hugged her back. "I like you, too."

Mary pulled away, then with another giggle and a conspiratorial look at Trey she trotted off to the bathroom.

Kara stood, shaken by the genuineness of the child's outburst of affection. Kids. She'd never had a clue around them, but Mary didn't seem to care. Maybe she should pass out pink T-shirts more often.

She caught Trey watching her. "I don't mind telling her how old I am. It's not like it's a secret."

"Take it from me, that's not where she was going with her question." He grimaced. "And don't ask."

She laughed at the chagrined look in his eyes. "Thanks for reminding me she was there a minute ago. I'd totally forgotten. She's so quiet."

"Sometimes." A smile tugged at his lips as he patted Missy's diapered bottom. She was barely keeping her eyes open now, her head nestling into the crook of his neck. "I've learned the hard way that unless I want my brother and sister-in-law to get a word-for-word replay of everything I say, I'd better be alert to a miniature undercover operative in my midst."

The sound of water running in the bathroom sink echoed into the expanse of the room. Outside the Warehouse, wind buffeted. Ice crystals pecked at the windows. A floorboard creaked.

"Kara—"

"Trey—"

They both stopped. He nodded toward her. "Ladies first." *Please God, get me through this.*

"I'm sorry for not telling everyone that you were watching movies with me that night. That you were nowhere near the Logan property when it caught on fire. When I heard you'd been accused, arrested—" She took a ragged breath, voice quavering as her tear-filled eyes sought his. "Can you ever forgive me?"

"Already did, darlin'," his low voice assured her. "A long time ago."

She stared at him. Not comprehending the kindness reflected in his eyes. Wasn't this where he was supposed to pull out his cell phone and dial 911? Report her for withholding evidence in a criminal case?

"I knew you were scared." His words washed over her in a reassuring wave. "Understood why you didn't want anyone to know you were with me. Especially your mom."

"I'm so sorry." But not for the reasons he thought. There was so much more to the story of that night that he didn't know. So much more that she couldn't tell. "If I could go back, as I've done ten thousand times in my mind, I'd do it all over again. But right, this time. I hate myself for what you had to go through."

"No need for that." His eyes grew thoughtful as if mentally traveling back in time. "I admit juvenile detention wasn't any fun. Or the unending community service projects. Or summer school so I could get my diploma. But I know now it could have been worse."

She tilted her head, hanging on his every word. "How could it have been worse?"

"I could have been eighteen, not just shy of it," he continued. "It could have been national forest service property instead of Duffy Logan's, a forgiving church member. And my dad could have been the town drunk instead of a respected pastor."

She clenched her fists in an effort to warm ice-cold

fingers. To stop their trembling. "Why didn't you rat me out? Make me come forward?"

He hadn't attempted to contact her in the days after his arrest. Not once.

"I knew you were mad at me, you know, for—" He swallowed. Glanced away.

"Having the guts to say no?" Heat burned her cheeks as the memory flared. How he'd responded to her kisses. At first. Then the look on his face when she made that inappropriate proposal. How he'd stepped back. Held her at arms' length. Apologized for getting carried away. Left without another word.

Don't deny his assumption. Let him think you sold him out to retain driving privileges and peace with your mom. Sold him out for childish revenge.

"It's all in the past." Gentle eyes echoed his smile. "Let's leave it there."

Wonder filled her. "Thank you."

Missy moved restlessly in his arms, and Kara took a step toward the door. She needed to get away. Come to terms with what had just transpired. At long last she'd apologized. And he'd forgiven. "I'd better let you get the girls to bed. But—"

There was one more thing she needed to know.

He shushed the little girl, who was beginning to fuss. "Yeah?"

"You never liked this town, even before the fire. Why did you come back?"

He took a breath. "Guess you might call it unfinished business."

She shook her head, not following his train of thought.

"Injury sidelined me from the rodeo circuit. Then I was hired to relaunch the Logan facility. Planned to get in and get out."

How was that old business? Restoring the place he'd been accused of torching?

"Reyna's been dogging me to stay on. To settle down here. A few months ago I'd have said no way." He gazed down at Missy cuddled in his arms. "But the place grows on you, you know? And with Missy and Mary... Well, I've decided to clear my name and call Canyon Springs home."

Her heart jolted. "How are you going to do that? Nobody's going to listen to me at this late date. Believe that I'm your alibi."

"You're right. And I won't ask you to do that. This isn't your battle. It's mine."

"Then how?"

"I have to prove myself to the community. That I'm a man of integrity. A man to be trusted." He glanced down at the again-dozing Missy. "You see, Kara, you're not the only person who didn't come forward. Someone else knows I didn't set that fire."

Kara's fists clenched in her pockets.

"One other person knows, because they started it. Left my cigarette lighter there. And I intend to find out who that person is."

"He's *what?*"

Kara clutched her mother's arm as she helped her

to the house's back door after church on Sunday. She'd hardly slept at all last night. No wonder, after Trey's bombshell. But surely she misunderstood what her mom said.

"You heard me, doll. Coming for lunch." Her mother grasped the railing to steady herself. "His nieces, too, of course."

Trey could be arriving any minute?

Last night he'd no more voiced his intention to find the real arsonist when Mary had trotted into the room to show off her T-shirt PJs. Avoiding Trey's gaze, Kara had oohed and aahed to the little girl's delight. Then made her escape.

But now this. Nowhere to run. Nowhere to hide.

Trey had forgiven her when he thought she'd just been a scared, stupid kid. One who immaturely reacted out of fear. Immature revenge. He had no idea she'd known this whole time who'd started the fire.

He'd hate her when he found out.

She held open the door to the enclosed porch for her mom, greeted by the tantalizing scent of a Crock-Pot pork roast and the lingering aroma of an apple pie baked earlier that morning. Mom knew that kind of thing wasn't on her doctor-mandated diet, but she'd stubbornly called the Warehouse yesterday afternoon and insisted Kara pick up the meat and other ingredients for a few of her many specialties. Said she felt like having company, which had long been a custom on Sundays before her late autumn heart attack. She'd always liked to see who God led her way to invite from church or the neighborhood.

But why Trey of all people?

When they'd divested themselves of coats and boots, they moved on into the kitchen where her mother laid out five plates and handed her a fistful of silverware.

"Kind of surprised you'd invite Trey Kenton, Mom." She kept her voice even as she arranged the utensils. Years ago Mom had expressly forbidden her to see him outside the church youth group activities. Not that she always obeyed. "I didn't even know he was in town until Friday night."

"Need to talk business with him."

"What kind of business?"

"Looks like he'll be renting the Warehouse apartment."

Several spoons slipped from her fingers and clattered to the hardwood floor. She knelt to pick them up with a trembling hand. She tossed the utensils into the sink, then opened a drawer for replacements. "Don't you think maybe we should have discussed this first?"

"Got to chattin' with him after you went off with Meg this morning. Returned Missy's mitten, by the way." Mom winked. "He says he's indebted to you. Missy had already lost another mitten on his watch this week. He's down to the last spare pair and figured he'd be answering to Reyna if at least one of them didn't turn up."

She gave her mother a weak smile. She should have returned the mitten herself so Mom wouldn't have had an excuse to strike up a conversation with him this morning.

"But, Mom, for years you haven't wanted to deal with the headaches renters can bring." She smoothed a turned-up corner of the tablecloth. "Don't forget, I won't be here much longer to oversee a rental. Run interference if things don't work out."

"Haven't forgotten." Mom opened a cabinet and pulled out a serving platter. "But he mentioned you'd let him and the girls stay there last night. One thing led to another and, well, it seemed like the right thing to do. Him being the pastor's brother and all."

"But if you've decided to rent, wouldn't it be better to get the word out to your friends first? See if they know a nice, quiet, local girl who'd put up pretty curtains and keep the place neat and clean? I don't want to sound biased, but most guys are notoriously bad housekeepers."

Mom was okay with some clutter but a stickler for cleanliness, so throwing out that reminder was worth a shot.

Her mother shrugged. "He's going to use it as an office, too, so I assume he'll keep it presentable."

"But Trey Kenton? Mom, don't you remember how you—"

"Boys grow up."

Now where had she heard that before?

Kara opened a cabinet and searched for two plastic

cups for the girls. No glassware for the wee ones. "You know what you always said about Dad. Cowboys ain't nothin' but trouble."

Her mother chuckled and dried her hands on the towel looped on the refrigerator door handle. "Guess I did say that a time or two, didn't I?"

"A time or two?" She stared in openmouthed disbelief. "It was a never-ending litany. You didn't want me to have anything to do with Trey even though he was the minister's son."

Her mother sobered as she opened the oven to peek in at the still-baking potatoes. "I was hurtin' bad back then, doll. Your dad leaving was a blow I wasn't prepared for. Takes time for even God to heal that kind of stuff."

"Sure, but—"

"Honey," her mom said, turning a frank gaze on her, "if you're afraid Trey might burn down the Warehouse, remember almost nobody accused him of deliberately catching fire to the forest. He was careless with a cigarette. But he doesn't smoke now. I made sure of that."

"It's not that, it's just—" She heard the rumble of a truck pulling around to the back of the house.

At the sound of an engine cutting off and the slam of a door, her mom handed her the salt and pepper shakers, then peeked out the window. "There they are. He sure seems to have those kids in tow quite a bit. I imagine that's one reason why he wants a place of his own in town. A little privacy."

So she *had* known Trey had been back awhile.

But why couldn't he rent a room at the Canyon Springs Inn? A cabin at Mackey's? There were plenty of available places in the off-season. Why did it have to be the Warehouse? She joined her mother at the window to watch as Trey opened the back passenger-side door and leaned in to unharness the girls.

Think of something. Fast.

"You know he has a dog, don't you?" Mom never liked animals in the house. Wouldn't even let her keep so much as a hamster indoors. "What's he going to do with that big hairy dog?"

"Says Rowdy's house-trained, so I assume he'll take him on walks. Forest service property is just a few blocks away."

Her stomach did a rollover. *Rowdy?* Mom knew his mutt's name?

This was not looking good.

"Is this Kara's house, Uncle Trey?"

Mary strained to see over his shoulder as he bent down to unbuckle her harness.

"Sure is."

"I think I like her house." She bobbed her head with deliberate motion to make the wispy five-inch-long ponytail swish from side to side.

That morning she'd insisted her hair be put in a ponytail. Couldn't be talked out of it. He'd finally found a rubber band in the back of a kitchen drawer, but it was no easy chore. Came out off center, but she didn't seem to mind.

He glanced toward the familiar cream-colored house nestled under a canopy of ponderosas. Like Mary, he liked the Dixon place. Or used to. Until the night he had to make the hardest decision he'd ever made up to that point in his young life. And for more nights than he cared to admit, he wondered if it had been the right one.

He refocused on his nieces, ignoring the tension in his upper arms. Man, Kara's mom used to scare him to death. Even now, fixing to walk up to her door seemed no less a feat of raw courage than when a chute gate swung open and a near-ton of horned, hard-as-steel muscle leaped out from under him and into an arena. He chuckled at the comparison. That facing Kara's mom on her home turf was akin to gearing up for a bone-jarring, neck-snapping, eight-second ride.

"Why are you laughing, Uncle Trey?"

He pulled the zipper of Mary's coat up to her neck. "'Cause your Uncle Trey is still a big, overgrown kid."

Mary giggled.

He'd been pretty proud of himself talking to Mrs. Dixon at the church earlier this morning. Managed to carry on a conversation like the adult he was. Joked about Missy's AWOL mitten. But when he thanked her for last night's use of the Warehouse, mentioned his interest in renting it, he hadn't anticipated she'd be so open to the idea. She had invited him to lunch for further discussion. Maybe his efforts at integrating into the community were paying off, too. He must have presented himself well. Proved he'd matured. Was reliable.

Either that or she was desperate for rent money.

"Get those girls in here, young man." Mrs. Dixon waved at him from where she'd poked her head out the open back porch door. "Freezing out there."

"Yes, ma'am." He tipped his hat in her direction, then helped Mary out of the backseat before reaching for Missy. He negotiated the shoveled-out walkway, passing by the door of a freestanding, two-car garage. Did Kara still have that classic '63 Ford Mustang in there? He'd have to check it out.

Inside the glass-paned porch, the enticing aroma of a hot-cooked meal greeted him. His stomach rumbled in anticipation. Except for a burger and fries at Kit's Lodge Friday evening and pizza at Meg's last night, he and his nieces had lived off soup and sandwiches the past several days. Cereal for breakfast.

It took some doing, but he got the girls and himself out of their winter wear, then joined Kara's mom in the kitchen. Did this room ever bring back memories. The white-painted cupboards, the wooden kitchen table with its ladder-back chairs, the faint scent of cinnamon. A still-familiar collection of sun catchers sparkled in the window. It was as if time had never passed.

"Go on in the living room, Trey." Mrs. Dixon waved

him toward the arched doorway. "Make yourself and the girls at home. I'll change clothes, then we can eat in about twenty minutes."

She disappeared down a hallway, and he ushered Mary in front of him as he carried Missy to the living room. Kara, in jeans and a rose-colored sweater, knelt by a stack of split logs in the tiled entryway. Gathering an armful, she glanced at him with an uncertain smile, but didn't seem surprised to see him. Her mom must have told her he was coming.

She stood and, as she turned, one of the logs clattered to the floor.

"Here, let me help with that." He set Missy down in a nearby rocker and crossed the room to reach for the armload of wood.

"Thanks." Her fair skin flushed as she relinquished it to him, then bent to pick up the stray log. When she straightened, her long-lashed gray eyes met his. And as always, the impact staggered him.

He swallowed. "Thanks for telling your mom about my interest in the apartment."

"Don't thank me. That was her idea."

"Maybe. But I got to thinking about what you said about her remembering me from high school. So knowing how she felt back then, you can't convince me you didn't put in a good word."

With effort, he dragged his gaze from hers, then moved across the room to kneel in front of the stone fireplace. He checked the damper and arranged the wood in the iron grate.

Kara held out a few fire starter wedges to him, her soft hand grazing his, and an unexpected jolt of electricity shot up his arm. Man, what was his problem? This was worse than it had been in high school. Acutely aware of her, he shifted away.

"Pretty clever means, *Pastor* Kenton," her lilting voice teased, "of getting out of a sermon at the worship service this morning."

He grinned. It *was* ingenious, if he said so himself. "Hey, Vannie's a talented guitar player. And Cassidy sings like an angel."

"And everyone loved seeing those teenagers up there leading a song service, so you scored points with the whole congregation."

"Aim to please."

Amusement glinted in her eyes as she gave him a multipurpose lighter, her hand again brushing his. In spite of the distraction, in a matter of minutes he had flames licking the wood. He stood, dusting off his hands. "There you go."

"Just like old times."

Their gazes met again. Old times. How had he forgotten the afternoon he'd once helped her get the fireplace going? How they'd knelt side by side, groaning when each time they lit the match, got the kindling in flames, it would go out. Bumping elbows. Playfully pushing. Each vying to see who could get it started first.

He recalled it now like yesterday. How she'd leaned her shoulder into his, wedged her way in front of him, deliberately whipping her ponytail in his face to divert him from their playful competition. In retaliation, he'd slipped his arms around her waist. Pulled her back. Back into his arms where she'd turned, her face brushing his cheek. Her eyes laughing into his, her mouth only inches...

That's when her mom had walked in, and from the look on her face he'd known he'd worn out his welcome. From then on he was no longer ushered into the heart of the Dixon household unless accompanied by friends. As their gazes now locked in shared memory, he knew he was in trouble. Big trouble.

But...would that be so bad? Now that they had their misunderstandings out in the open? Could begin to relate to each other as adults? Maybe that was teenage foolishness, him still thinking he needed to steer clear of her. She'd apologized last night. Sounded plenty sincere, too. The tears in her eyes had about done him in.

Sure was a pretty little gal. All soft and good-smelling. Even his nieces liked her. Couldn't keep their eyes off her any more than he could. Maybe it wasn't *only* to prove his innocence that God had opened doors for a return to Canyon Springs?

He cleared his throat. Couldn't let his mind wander down that road right now. Get his hopes up only to get the stuffings knocked out of him again. "I guess—"

The crash of ceramic hitting the entryway tile sent them both whipping around.

Chapter Six

"Oh, Missy!" His older, ponytailed niece pushed the startled two-year-old away from the pottery fragments littering the tiles. "Look what you did."

He frowned. Missy? No way could the toddler have reached up on the bookcase to pull a piece of Navajo pottery from its perch. But a four-year-old could.

He moved to kneel between the two girls, reaching out to block Missy from moving closer to the shards. She stared at the broken object, not comprehending what had happened. But at least she didn't cry as Kara led her across the room.

He slipped an arm around Mary's waist and gave her a hug. "You okay?"

She nodded emphatically, avoiding his gaze.

"Care to tell me what happened?"

With flustered movements, she pointed to the shattered pieces. "She, she—"

"She?"

Mary nodded. "Uh-huh. She didn't mean to do it, Uncle Trey. It slipped."

He pulled her in close to whisper in her ear. "You're sure it was Missy?"

She nodded, her soft hair brushing his face. Man, he hated her lying to him. When *anyone* lied to him, for that matter. He turned her to face him and brushed back dark curls that had come loose from her ponytail, framing the pretty little face. "You know I count on you to always tell me the truth, princess."

He glanced over at Kara, who still kept Missy occupied, and her eyes met his. Great. Her expression looked almost as stricken as Mary's. He could replace the pottery's dollar value, but not if it had a sentimental one.

A soft sob from his older niece drew his attention. Lower lip trembling, a tear trickled down a flawless cheek.

He ran a reassuring hand along her arm. "You have something you want to tell me?"

Face crumpling, she flung herself into his arms and sobbed into his shoulder. "I did it, Uncle Trey. I didn't mean to. I was holding it tight. I didn't mean to. I'm sorry."

An ache deep inside swelled as her tiny warm body clung to him for all she was worth. She and Missy were his heart's pride and joy. How'd they manage to worm their way in there so quickly? Got him thinking that clearing his name and elbowing his way back into Canyon Springs was an answer to his prayers?

When the tears subsided, he pulled a handkerchief from his back pocket and dried her face. Let her blow her nose. Sad brown eyes gazed into his. "I'm sorry, Uncle Trey."

"You're forgiven." He gave her another hug, then pulled back to study her. "Remember, you can always tell me the truth. You don't ever need to lie to me, okay?"

She nodded.

"Now you need to tell Kara you're sorry, too."

He gave her a little nudge to where Kara stood by Missy. The toddler's arms were outstretched to her, indicating she wanted to be picked up, but Kara hadn't taken the hint.

Hands clasped behind her back, the voice of his older niece quavered. "I'm sorry, Kara."

"I know you are." Kara knelt and Mary hurried forward for a hug.

Trey stood. "Sorry about the pottery. I'll replace it if it can be replaced."

"Don't worry about it." Mrs. Dixon's voice came from across the room. "Just a piece I bought from a roadside stand up on the Rez. Didn't cost much."

He glanced again at Kara for confirmation, but she didn't meet his gaze. Deliberately avoided it, if he were any judge. But why'd that avoidance weigh so heavily on his heart? Why'd he long for her to smile up at him, to let him know she felt the same connection he was feeling?

But maybe she wasn't feeling it, too.

* * *

Never lie to me.

Trey's soft, measured words to his niece echoed through Kara's mind throughout the entire meal as he and her mother chatted amiably like old pals. Came to an agreement about renting the empty Warehouse space.

You know I count on you to always tell me the truth.

No doubt where he stood on that issue. When she'd apologized last night and he'd forgiven her, her heart had soared. Even praised God for hearing her for a change. But no more. Trey only forgave her for a partial truth.

"Kara?" Mary pushed her plastic cup toward her with a shy smile. "Can I have more milk?"

"Please," Trey reminded her as he cut Missy's meat. Always as well prepared as any Girl Scout, Mom had produced a booster seat from who knows where for the toddler.

"Please?" Mary echoed, then propped her chin on fisted hands and swished her hair from side to side. "Do you like my ponytail, Kara?"

"I sure do." She reached for the cup and filled it halfway from the jug next to her.

"Uncle Trey did it." The little girl cut a look at her uncle. "He wanted it to be like yours."

"You wanted it to be like Kara's," he corrected as he wiped Missy's face, then cast Kara an apologetic glance. "I did the best I could. Didn't have a ribbon."

"I can get you a ribbon after lunch."

Mary's eyes brightened as she reached out for her cup. "She's got a ribbon for me, Uncle Trey."

"That's what I hear. And what do we say when someone does something nice for us?"

"We say thank you." Mary clasped her hands in her lap. "But I don't have it yet."

"She has a point there, Trey." Kara's mom chuckled. "You may have a budding lawyer on your hands."

He shook his head, a smile tugging at his lips.

"And speaking of legalities," her mother continued, "I'll have the rental paperwork drawn up by the end of the week. But if you need to move anything in before then, go right ahead."

Why was she being so accommodating? Maybe, like her daughter, she was feeling guilty? Feeling bad because she'd all but outlawed him from the house? Now with him being the current pastor's brother, she felt she needed to make it up to him?

Trey excused himself from the table, then disappeared into the enclosed porch. A moment later he returned carrying the pink pom-pom key chain Meg had passed on to him last night.

"Now that it's almost official, does anyone mind if I switch this out for something less feminine?"

His laughing gaze caught Kara's and she couldn't help but smile back. He was such a decent, goodhearted guy. Which made her hate herself even more.

His kindness last night had freaked her out almost as much as his declaration that he intended to expose the real fire starter.

Trey glanced at his watch. "Almost time to give that devotion at the care facility. But thanks again for agreeing to the rental. And for inviting us for this award-winning meal."

Her mom stood and moved to the other side of the table to pick up Missy. Should she be doing that? Lifting that much weight?

"What are you going to do with the girls?" Mom gave the child a kiss on the cheek. "They aren't letting youngsters in at the care facility. No one under eighteen. Flu precaution."

Trey frowned. "Jason didn't mention that."

"Heard it was announced Friday. Leave 'em here. We'll find ourselves a book. Flake out together for a nap."

"You're sure, Mrs. Dixon? I might be able to—"

"Yes, I'm sure. The Pastor For A Day is entitled to a few perks. And," she added, "my name's Sharon."

Inwardly Kara groaned. Why was Mom taking such a shine to Trey? This was a bit extreme even if she'd been overcome with belated guilt.

"All right. Thanks. And Sharon it is." Trey picked up his and Missy's plates. "I can help clean up here. That's the least I can do for you ladies after such a fine meal."

"I'll take care of it." Kara took the plates from him.

Mom waved her away. "Just put everything in the

sink to soak. You used to do Sunday visits at Pine Country with me. Trey could probably use some help. Show him the ropes. Play that piano pretty for them."

Thanks a lot, Mom. She had a ton of things to do this afternoon. Needed to check on Roxanne at the Warehouse. Spend some time in front of the computer catching up on Garson Design business. She hadn't spent much time this past week on the new project. What if Spence called to ask about its status?

Trey caught her eye. "You don't have to go. I imagine they'll take pity on me and not start any riots when Jason doesn't show up."

"Kara needs to get out," Mom insisted. "She's spent the last month cooped up with me or at the Warehouse."

"Actually, Mom, I—"

From behind Trey, her mom shook her head, a death ray all but shooting from her eyes. Why was she—? A cold chill spiraled up her spine.

A family-style meal. Renting the apartment. Babysitting his nieces. A warm welcome to the man she'd once warned Kara away from.

Was Mom trying to fix her up with Trey—to keep her from leaving Canyon Springs?

Self-consciously aware of his proximity, Kara gave Trey a furtive glance as they pulled out of the driveway to head to Pine Country Care. His pickup fishtailed as it momentarily fought for traction in the freshly plowed street, then straightened. Snow crunched under the tires in a soothing rhythm.

What she'd have given twelve years ago to have been openly riding through town beside him. With the handsome new boy. With somebody everybody didn't think they already knew everything about. What must it be like to grow up where everyone didn't know you from your diaper days? Didn't know you'd fallen off your bike on the way to school in third grade. That you'd bombed on middle school cheerleading tryouts. That your first date stood you up.

Didn't know your dad had run off and left you behind.

A neighbor drew her attention as he paused from shoveling his driveway for a friendly wave. She and Trey waved back, and from the satisfied look on Trey's face this was a hometown perk he liked. The recognition. Friendliness. But she imagined they wouldn't reach their destination before it would be all over Canyon Springs that they'd been spotted together. One of the many joys of small towns she'd be happy to do without.

She settled back in her seat and sneaked another peek at Trey. Despite his relaxed, smiling expression, tension tightened in her forearms. Now was the time to learn how he planned to uncover the real fire starter. If she didn't draw him out, there was no telling when she'd again have the opportunity.

"Meg said you're taking Vannie Quintero on to mentor. Sort of a youth coach. You're serious about this clearing your name and winning over the old hometown, aren't you?"

Trey nodded, keeping his eyes on the snow-packed road. "You bet. I'm also assisting with an affordable housing project. Sort of a Habitat for Humanity kind of thing. Donating supplies to fix up the local youth center, too."

She forced an encouraging smile. Put a teasing lilt in her tone. "Kind of overkill, isn't it, cowboy?"

He returned her smile with a genuine one of his own. "I can't move back here if I don't get the business up and running by summer, and to do that I need to gain the respect and cooperation of the community. As it is, one of the city officials is giving me the run-around. I can't believe how much authority is granted to city councilmen here."

"Small-town bureaucracy. Get used to it." She tucked a loose strand of hair under her faux fur hat. "So why not go where nobody knows you? Where you don't have to prove anything to anyone. Start fresh."

"Believe me, this wasn't my idea." He shook his head, wonder reflecting in his eyes. "God's been opening doors and nudging me through them."

Kara laughed. "Boy, am I glad God's not as hands-on in my life as He is in yours. No way would I voluntarily move back here. He'd have to drag me back kicking and screaming."

He shot her a questioning look. "I don't know which surprises me most. That you don't like Canyon

Springs—or that you don't believe God's involved in your life."

"Well, He's not involved like He is in yours, apparently."

"What makes you think that?"

"Don't get me wrong. I totally believe in God. Joined His team when I was ten." She remembered well the preschool and thereafter days when Mom dropped her off for kids' programs on Sundays. Neither of her folks were into anything having to do with God back then, but it made a convenient day care one morning a week. "It's just that when Dad left and didn't come back, I realized God answers some people's prayers, but not others. I'm one of the not others."

Trey frowned, but it appeared he was smart enough not to argue. She turned to look out the side window as they drove through what passed in Canyon Springs for a downtown. Hovering at a population of just under three thousand, the off-the-beaten-path community nestled in the pines. Like her mother's general store, most shops were geared to luring in seasonal visitors. Bikers, hikers, campers and fishermen in the summer. Cross-country skiers and other lovers of winter sports during the snow-packed months. The place certainly looked quaint enough on a day like this, with a frosty layer on the ground and clinging to pine branches.

A nice place to visit, but…

Whoever would have thought a sensible guy like Trey would naively believe coming back to Canyon

Springs was a God thing? "In my estimation, Trey, hometowns are highly overrated. People build up this cozy little fantasy about them, but they don't deliver."

He mustered a smile. "I can see how the attraction is hard to explain to someone who's had a hometown to come back to."

"So you've bought into the Mitford myth?"

"What's that?"

"You know, the glory, laud and honor hymn wistfully sung to small-town America."

Trey chuckled. "There's a lot to be said for a sense of belonging. Roots."

"Lots to be said for independence, too." She met his gaze in challenge. "Wings."

With an indulgent smile, he turned down another pine-lined side street, a hodgepodge mix of A-frames and ranch-style homes with roofs, decks and porch rails softened by a layer of white. "So you see those two values—roots and wings—as polar opposites? They can't complement and support each other?"

"Not here. Stick around and you'll see what I mean."

Canyon Springs probably did seem pretty idyllic compared to his on-the-road rodeo lifestyle. And he'd moved around a lot growing up, too, with his folks starting churches and filling in at small-town congregations that couldn't afford a full-time pastor. But life here would only disappoint him in the long run.

As they rounded another corner just inside the city

limits, her startled gaze flew to the barren expanse of Duffy Logan's old horse property. The land where Trey was renovating the long-neglected equine facility.

The site of the fire.

Even now, a dozen years later, five once-forested acres stood barren except for blackened, knee-high stumps where the damaged trees had been cut down for safety's sake. They pushed up out of the snow like flat-topped shark's fins. Silent sentinels, witnesses to the foolishness of her past.

She cut a look at Trey. He came here every day. Drove past it, then down the winding lane through the thick stand of remaining trees to the indoor arena and stables. Maybe he was used to seeing it by now, but she'd avoided the area all these years. Even now it made her sick to her stomach to look at it.

To her dismay, he slowed the truck in front of the barren stretch of land. "I've got a guy scheduled to come in here this spring to pull out all the stumps."

She twisted her gloved hands. "What will you use the land for?"

"Parking possibly. Or another workout arena. Maybe just pasture. Whatever we decide on, at least we'll clear out the remnants of the fire."

"I'm surprised nobody's already done that." Did her voice sound as wooden to him as it did to her own ears?

"It's not going to be cheap to clear it out, grade it, make sure it's contoured for good drainage. Fence it in. Duffy wouldn't have had the money for that. Then after his stroke, the property sat here, neglected. You know he died a few years ago, don't you?"

"Yeah. He'd think it was great you're fixing the place up. What are you going to call it?"

"High Country Equine Center." He gave her a lop-sided grin. "But I imagine locals will always call it Duffy's. You want to see it?" He braked the truck as they neared a double-wide entrance marked by two stone posts and a wrought-iron arch.

"Right now, you mean?"

Trey glanced at the dashboard clock. "Guess not, huh? Time for our visit. But afterward, maybe? Or some other time."

"Maybe another time." Nervous fingers toyed with the cuff of her sleeve. "Have a lot going on today."

"You've probably been to Duffy's before, right? So I think you'll appreciate the changes we're making." His voice held a note of pride. "Gutted the main stable section adjoining the arena and have redone that. Tore down peripheral buildings that had seen better days, too. Will replace those as time and money allow. Remodeling the office next."

He applied his foot to the gas pedal again, and three-quarters of a mile farther down the tree-lined road pulled the pickup into the plowed parking lot of Pine Country Care. A low-slung building with a steep-pitched roof, it hunkered down in the frozen expanse beneath a stand of ponderosa pines.

As they walked up the paved pathway to the facility,

Trey touched her arm. "Thanks for helping me today. I felt like your mom kind of badgered you into it."

"She wants me to get out more. Thinks I've been pushing myself too hard since I came back."

And that if she throws me at you, Trey, I'll return for good. Not.

He opened the wooden double door at the entrance and, smiling her thanks, she stepped forward. Then stopped. For right in front of her, bundled up against the cold, stood the person she least expected, but most needed, to see.

Her cousin, Lindi Bruce. Not looking in the least bit happy.

Chapter Seven

With a quick "Hi, cuz," Kara stepped inside to give Lindi a hug. But her longtime friend didn't return it with much enthusiasm.

Trey joined them in the spacious lobby and Lindi, her dark brown hair glinting in the soft light, arched a delicate brow. "Surprised to see you two here."

Meaning together.

"Trey's brother," Kara said, not wanting her cousin to jump to conclusions, "is the pastor at Canyon Springs Christian. He got snowed out of town. So Trey's filling in and Mom wants me to show him the ropes. So, what brings you here? Nobody in the family's ill, I hope."

"No." Lindi glanced around the lobby, then lowered her voice. "Checking in on my future senior constituency."

"She's running for city councilman. Woman. Person." Kara jumped in to clarify for Trey. "Youngest in the city's history, if she gets elected."

Lindi straightened the handbag slung over her jacketed shoulder. "Uncle Ed's retired and Grandpa's ready to, but since no one else in the family wants to pick up where they left off, it falls to me to keep the family name in the city annals."

"And your grandfather is—?" Trey ventured.

He wouldn't have paid much attention to local politics as a teenager, know Lindi's connections. But he'd mentioned a city official giving him a hard time, hadn't he? That sounded a lot like the man who'd raised Lindi when her father and mother—Kara's mom's sister—had been killed in a car accident.

"City Councilman Reuben Falkner," the young candidate spoke with evident pride.

Trey nodded agreeably enough, but Kara noticed the hairbreadth lowering of his brows. A flicker in his eyes. Even after all these years she could tell something about the name of Lindi's grandfather had struck home in a not-so-pleasant fashion.

"City Council will take up a lot of time," Lindi continued. "Time I'd prefer to devote to my family and catering business, but how can I say no to Grandpa?"

Although she smiled, she wasn't joking. Nobody said no to her grandpa. While the council bylaws limited the length of an individual position to three years, that didn't stop anyone from running for office every other election. Councilman Falkner and his brother believed that as descendants of the community's founders they had a responsibility to govern.

"We need to get set up for the worship service." Kara caught Trey's eye, then turned to give Lindi a pointed look. "I'll be in touch. *Soon*."

An hour and a half later, with a devotional, extended time of singing and a few dozen hugs behind them, Kara and Trey headed home.

Trey carefully steered the pickup around a four-foot high berm of snow left by a plow at one end of Kara's street. "I thought things went well, didn't you?"

"They're always so appreciative of visits." She tossed back her ponytail. "But I can't believe you were asking Mr. Manter all those questions afterward."

"I told you I intend to clear my name."

"By interrogating some poor old man?"

"He was the vice principal of the high school back then. Don't you remember? Knew all the kids. Knows the town."

"But still—"

"I've been in and out of Canyon Springs the past year, semi-living here since September, and no one's come forward with tips or a confession. So I'm stepping it up a bit. Need to be more aggressive."

"I thought you wanted to worm your way into everyone's heart. Earn their respect. But asking a bunch of questions, making accusations—" Townspeople wouldn't like random finger-pointing. Unfounded allegations. They wouldn't like *him*. She had to put a stop to it before this went any further and caused even greater damage to his reputation. She couldn't just stand by and watch. Not a second time.

Trey pulled into the driveway next to Kara's mom's house and cut the engine. "I haven't made any accusations. I'm investigating."

She reached for the door handle. Maybe she could talk him out of further probing until she got things settled once and for all with Lindi. "It's going to get around that you're snooping. People won't like that."

"You don't understand why this is so important to me, do you?" His solemn gaze held hers. "Why I can't let it go."

"You could do yourself more harm than good." She opened the door, but before she could get out, he laid his hand on her arm.

"Then tell me you'll help me, Kara."

From the look on her face, you'd have thought he'd asked her to help him dispose of a body. The dread in her eyes told him all he needed to know. What he'd begun to suspect. Disappointment plunged a saber into his soul.

"You're not sure that I didn't set that fire, are you?"

With a quick intake of breath, her eyes widened. "What? No, no, Trey, I never thought that."

"You're thinking I could have started it before I came by your place. That it smoldered and flamed to life later that night."

She placed her hand over his, her grip tightening

as her beautiful eyes pleaded. "That never crossed my mind. Ever."

"So you will help me?"

"I—"

The distress in her gaze belied the words of assurance. He'd thought all this time that she hadn't come forward because she'd been humiliated by his rejection. It never occurred to him she doubted his innocence.

"I didn't start that fire, Kara." He took a ragged breath and reached for his own door handle. He needed to retrieve the girls. Pick up Rowdy from Meg. Get out of here.

Her grip tightened again on his arm, her gaze intent. "I believe you, Trey. One hundred percent. But you already agreed no one would buy me as your belated alibi."

Hope sparked. "This is your hometown. You grew up here. You know everybody or know somebody who does. We can figure it out together."

"Don't you think your time would be better invested in your business? It'll bring a positive economic impact to the community. That's what will win the town to your side."

"It's not enough." *Please, Lord, it's important that she understand.* "Twelve years is a long time to live knowing no one believed me when I said I didn't do it. No one except my family."

"Nobody said you set the fire on purpose. Accidents happen."

"An accident didn't happen." His jaw tightened. "Someone tossed down a cigarette—and my lighter. It may not have been set deliberately, but someone implicated me. If it happened to you, wouldn't you wonder what you'd done to make someone want to get back at you like that? Want answers? Justice?"

"Whoever found your lost lighter may not even have known who it belonged to."

Maybe. But it had been distinctive. Silver with a turquoise stone embedded in the side. He gazed at her a long moment, a heaviness settling in his chest.

"I thought you'd understand. I mean, you took a lot of hassle about your dad." Guilt stabbed that he couldn't yet tell her about his connection to her father. "So you know what it feels like to be talked about."

"I know it doesn't feel good. Believe me, I haven't forgotten the time you stepped in when those kids were giving me a hard time. Speculating about what my father had done. Why he left Mom and me behind."

Why hadn't he thought of it before? "That's it."

"What?"

"Those kids. The ones I set straight. What were their names?"

Her expression darkened. "You're way off track. They were good kids basically. Just misguided."

"But it makes sense, doesn't it? That they'd want to get back at me?" He marveled that the answer had been there right in front of his face all this time. "I only went to school here a handful of months, so the names and faces are blurry. Was it Gord? Cord? What was the kid's name—the chubby one with the braces? You know who I'm talking about."

"He goes by Cordell now," she said with obvious reluctance. "He's a police officer."

"Like cops never did anything stupid when they were kids? And he had a couple of sidekicks. Little goth gal. Black hair. Purple sparkle nail polish. Tattoo on the back of her neck."

"Lark. She's a social worker for the county. Both have made decent lives for themselves."

"Of course they did." His voice hardened. "And they could do it because they weren't looked on with suspicion."

"Trey—"

"There were a couple of others, weren't there? Work with me here, Kara."

She looked him square in the eye. "No. If you want to win the community's favor, accusing some of its reputable citizens isn't the way to go about it."

"I told you I'm not accusing anyone."

"But the plan is to eventually, isn't it?" Her gray eyes wide with an alarm he didn't understand, she leaned toward him. "Do yourself a favor, Trey. Don't."

"I want a ponytail again." Mary pushed away her empty cereal bowl. "Like Kara."

"Kara who?" her mother asked, wiping the Wednesday breakfast table with a damp cloth.

"Uncle Trey's Kara."

Trey jerked his head up from where he'd had his nose buried in yesterday's newspaper, barely listening to the girlish conversation going on around him. What had she just said?

"Uncle Tway! Uncle Tway!" Missy banged the flat of her hand on the table.

"Uncle Trey has a Kara, does he?" Reyna raised her brows and glanced in his direction. "Interesting."

He scowled. "No, it's not interesting. So get that gleam out of your eyes. Kara Dixon has a ponytail and Mary's taken a liking to it."

Reyna laughed. "And why does that make you so cranky this morning?"

He shot her a warning glare. He wasn't cranky. He just didn't want her breathing down his neck. Pushing him at Kara the way she'd done Meg. She often pointed out that if he hadn't dragged his feet when he had first met the cute schoolteacher, it might not be her cousin walking Meg down the aisle in March.

Mary slid out of her chair and trotted around to him. "Uncle Trey?"

He focused on his pajama-clad niece. "What, princess?"

"You like ponytails, don't you?" She patted his arm. "And kissing?"

"Kissing?" Reyna laughed again. "By all means, Uncle Trey, please share the answer to that one."

He folded the paper, placed it on the table and stood. Almost tripped over Rowdy snoozing at his feet. "Talk to your mom about ponytails, Mary. The only ponytails I know anything about are on the back end of a pony."

He could still hear Missy's "Uncle Tway" chant and the threesome's giggles as he snatched his jacket and hat off hooks by the back door. He headed out with Rowdy into the still-dark morning to feed his horses. Now he'd never hear the end of this ponytail thing from Reyna. She'd dog him about her old high school classmate at every opportunity. The very thing he didn't need right now. Not with the way things ended with Kara Sunday.

So much for toying with the idea that God might have a happily ever after plan in the works there. Not only could she hardly wait to get out of Canyon Springs, but she thought his quest for justice would backfire on him. And her talk about God not being involved in her life? A red light for sure.

He slipped into the ice-cold, two-stall barn where his two American quarter horses, Taco and Beamer, had come in from the adjoining corral when they'd heard his approach. They headed into their respective stalls, waiting patiently for him to fill their feed buckets. Within minutes the barn echoed with contented horse sighs, swishing tails and the soothing sound of his equine friends rummaging in their buckets and chewing grain. He located a currycomb and, with Rowdy watching from the doorway, went to work on Taco.

It was plenty clear the root of Kara's beliefs about

God stemmed from her dad's unwise choices. He'd known her father since his own early days on the rodeo circuit, when her dad was into rodeo promotion, not participation. And as Leonard "Dix" Dixon himself had explained it to him when Trey'd been chosen by the investors group to run Duffy's old place, he'd left rodeoing to settle down and raise a family. But he hadn't prepared well for that transition. Too restless. Wasn't cut out to be a shopkeeper at Dix's Woodland Warehouse.

Eventually, against his wife's objections, he'd been lured by an old acquaintance into a "sure thing" opportunity to make a killing off real estate speculation in the boom days of hotter-than-hot land deals in the West. Apparently the amiable, likable Dix, with all good intentions, sweet-talked trusting locals into investing with him. But he didn't have the experience or the business savvy needed, and promising deal after deal fell through. Cost his investors thousands. Turned more than a few local residents against him. Was the last straw that busted up his marriage to one of the town's favorite sweethearts. And under a cloud of shame, he'd left Sharon and thirteen-year-old Kara behind.

Which is why Dix didn't want his name mentioned as one of the equine center's investors. He'd come into some money in a later remarriage and wanted to invest it anonymously back into the community he'd let down. But that was something Trey needed to talk to him about now that Kara was home. Didn't sit right to keep it from her. As much as he himself hated deception, he didn't like being a part of Dix's.

Rowdy brushed up against Trey's leg, bringing him back to the present. As troubling as he found the situation with Dix, Kara's reaction to his plan for vindication disturbed him as well. Were both she and Jason right? Had he misread why circumstances led him back to Canyon Springs? Was seeking to be exonerated a fool's errand he'd live to regret?

"She denied ever thinking I set the fire, Rowdy," he said aloud. "Sounded convincing enough. But maybe she thinks I'd blame someone else just to get out from under this cloud."

Trey scratched Taco behind the ear, his mind's eye drifting back through the years. A once-in-a-lifetime opportunity with the pretty teenager had presented itself that night and he'd turned it down flat. Even as enjoyable as the prelude had been, he'd known in the back of his mind she was acting out. Getting back at her mom. Her dad.

Shoving away the too-vivid memory, he gave Taco's winter-coated sides another round with the curry-comb. "Don't know where I got the strength to get myself out of there, guys. Must have been the good Lord whispering in my ear." He chuckled. "Either that or my healthy fear of Sharon Dixon."

But all joking aside, he still had the here-and-now Kara to deal with. And steering clear seemed the best plan of action.

Chapter Eight

"You haven't forgotten your promise, have you?" Kara's cousin Lindi Bruce whispered from where she sat across the polished wooden table at Kit's Lodge.

Kara drew her gaze from the window. The winter morning stood out in stark contrast to the warm, rustic interior of the lodging and eating establishment. Even with a sparse morning crowd, she was comfortable that their conversation wouldn't be overheard above the breakfast chatter.

"I haven't forgotten. There's not a day that goes by when I'm back here that I'm not reminded of it."

She studied her cousin. Unbelievably, they hadn't talked about the promise since they were teenagers. Hadn't discussed the morning a terrified Lindi appeared on her doorstep, confessing she'd accidentally caught the forest on fire. Begging Kara not to tell, not to get her in trouble with her grandfather—or the law.

By unspoken agreement, they'd attempted to bury

it so deeply that for a time they could all but convince themselves it never happened. That they'd dreamed it. But it was still very much alive, like a giant gorilla stuffed in the closet of both their lives. And since Trey's return, it rattled the bars of its cage with increasing frequency and forcefulness.

"How about you, Lindi? How often do you think about it?"

"Not much," she admitted. "Until each time you come back to visit. And now Trey. Freaked me out when I saw you with him."

"That's why I wanted to talk to you." Kara wet her lips. "He's determined to clear his name."

Lindi stiffened, her fork halfway to her mouth. "You haven't told him anything, have you?"

"No." Nor did she intend to mention that Trey asked her to advise him on what he called his investigation.

"What are we going to do?" Lindi set down her fork. "What if he puts two and two together? I was a smoker back then. At the very least I could be added to the list of suspects."

"You honestly want to know what I think we should do?"

Lindi nodded, interest sparking in her eyes.

"Come clean."

"What? Are you crazy?"

Kara met her cousin's look of alarm with determination. It wouldn't be easy to convince her, but there was no other way out. Even as she contemplated the difficult path ahead, a flutter of hope, the nearness of release, convinced her this was the right thing to do.

"We were both kids back then, Lin. Scared kids. Making that promise, keeping my mouth shut while Trey took the rap when they found his lighter—that *you* dropped—wasn't the smartest decision I've ever made. In fact, it was flat-out wrong."

The pitiful-little-girl look that had worked to Lindi's advantage for too many years to count focused on her full force.

"Do you have any idea what the fallout would be for me?"

"There's been fallout for Trey, too."

Lips compressed, Lindi again picked up her fork and stabbed a pineapple wedge. "Grandpa would have a heart attack if this came out in the middle of the campaign."

"Lindi—"

"It's not just about me." Her cousin cut a look around the room, then leaned forward. "If Jake Talford wins, he'll turn this town on its head. He's running on an economic growth platform that could destroy the way of life we've all come to love."

That *some* had come to love.

But although she didn't agree that Jake was such a danger to the community, she couldn't argue with her. A revelation that the natural-resource-protection-touting Lindi Bruce had not only set the forest on fire but kept her mouth shut and let someone else take the fall for it would be just the edge Jake needed.

"I know you have the town's best interests at heart, but—"

"What happened is in the past, Kara. What's done is done."

"There was a time when I wanted to believe that. But we can't let this go on any longer."

With shaking fingers, Lindi again set aside her fork, the pineapple still impaled on its tines. A fleeting cast of emotions flitted across her face. Indecision. Panic. Fear.

"There's more at stake here," she said, voice quavering, "than the city council spot."

The muscles in Kara's stomach tightened.

"James and I—" Lindi momentarily closed her eyes as if gathering courage. "Things are rocky, to say the least. Adding to it, he wants to take a job in Phoenix. But I don't want to raise the kids in the fifth largest city in the country. If we can't work things out, it will likely lead to divorce. And an ugly custody fight."

An invisible rope tightened around Kara's throat.

Lindi's tear-filled eyes bored into hers. "Do you know what all this coming out right now would do to my chances of getting sole custody of Craig and Kirk? I could forget it, that's what."

With her cousin's words, Kara's hope of freedom from the decade-long deception crashed with reverberating finality.

"I'm sorry, Lindi. I didn't know you were having

marriage problems." She leaned forward with a final desperate appeal. "But don't you see? We can't continue to let Trey be blamed."

"*We* can't? Or you can't?" Lindi pulled a tissue from her handbag and dabbed at her eyes. "You probably had a thing for him in high school, didn't you? All the girls did."

Kara's throat tightened. She pushed back her plate. "We were friends."

"But finding him here again, you'd like it to be more than friends, wouldn't you?"

"I'm leaving town a week from Monday," she said, ignoring the probing question. "Seeing Trey again— realizing how what we did is still affecting his life— well, it's killing me."

"Then run off to your big-city fantasyland and forget about it. This isn't your home now. Stop dwelling on the past."

"Believe me, I've tried."

Balling the tissue in her hand, Lindi lowered her voice to an almost inaudible level. "You know, don't you, that we could wind up in jail? At the least, he'd probably sue me. You, too."

They'd been well under eighteen. Minors. What was the statute of limitations on covering up a crime?

Lindi's eyes narrowed with a speculative gleam. "And what do you think this out-of-the-blue revelation would do to your mother's fragile state of health?"

Kara thrust the alarming thought of her mother

aside. "I want to be free, Lindi. I'd like your permission to tell Trey the truth."

"Well, you're not getting it. Haven't you been listening to anything I've said? What this could do to me?" Her friend pulled the napkin from her lap and slapped it down beside her plate. "You're not even thinking straight. You're letting a slow, lazy smile and flirty blue eyes trip you up."

"I can tell him without your permission, you know."

"No, I don't think you will." Tear-wet eyes triumphant, Lindi's trembling lips formed a faint smile. "You made a promise. And you don't want to be like your old man who couldn't keep one."

As she parked in the Canyon Springs Christian Church lot late that afternoon, a troubled Kara continued to mull over Lindi's words. The waitress at Kit's Lodge had stepped up just as Lindi had risen from her seat, so the breakfast conversation was terminated abruptly. Lindi even stuck her with the tab. How had their friendship deteriorated to this? All because of that stupid adolescent promise.

She dashed across the tree-lined street to the parsonage, then slowed down. This wasn't a Chicago thoroughfare where she had to dodge packs of pedestrians and impatient drivers. No reason to hurry around here, that was for certain.

Maneuvering around an SUV in the driveway as well as a car she recognized as Meg's, she entered the open garage door of the ranch-style house. A week or so ago her college friend, who was serving on the parsonage makeover committee, had brought her here for input on ideas she thought Reyna might like. They brainstormed together, did sketches, took measurements. So this is where she'd most likely left her tape measure.

But the missing device was the least of her problems. What was she going to do about Lindi? Yes, she could defy her cousin, break her promise and tell Trey the truth so he'd call a halt to his investigation. But that still seemed wrong. How well did she really know the grown-up Trey? What if he wouldn't keep silent? Wouldn't protect Lindi at the expense of his own reputation? The potential loss of the council seat didn't much matter to her, but could Lindi land in jail? Lose custody of her kids?

The door connecting the garage to the house was unlocked, so she slipped through the laundry room and into the kitchen. A radio in an adjoining room belted out an old toe-tapping country tune she hadn't heard in years. A night out at the symphony had become the preferred melodic choice. Still, she caught herself humming along to the familiar rhythm.

"Yoo hoo, Bryce! Meg! It's me, Kara."

She gazed around the kitchen in appreciation of Meg's earlier efforts. It was coming along nicely. Appliances had arrived since her last visit. Glass-fronted cabinets were now installed. Matching oak trimmed the granite countertop.

It reminded her of her mother's house, not so much because of the layout or color scheme, but the atmosphere. So cheery with sunlight spilling in the windows, playing across a caramel-colored accent wall. Cozy. Made you want to sit down at the as-yet-nonexistent table in the roomy new bay window and have a cup of coffee. A chat with a friend. Your spouse.

The image of Trey seated for breakfast flashed through her mind. Long, jeans-clad legs stretched out under the table. Booted feet. Broad shoulders squared as he brought a steaming mug of coffee to his lips...

With considerable effort, she refocused on the space around her. Unlike the palace-size interiors she'd helped design or decorate, this one was peo-ple-size. People-friendly. For more families than she cared to think about, the decision to build or buy seemed based on ensuring more than enough rooms to keep family members as far apart as possible. The economic slump might not be good for the design and construction business, but downsizing might do wonders for family dynamics. Not, of course, that a cute and cozy house had made one ounce of differ-ence in her own family's case.

Thanks, Dad.

"Hey, Kara." Bryce Harding, who was supervis-ing the remodel in his free time, stepped into the room. Like her, he'd grown up in Canyon Springs. But unlike her, he'd chosen to come back. "What brings you here today?"

She smiled at the bearded, lovable bear of a man in his mid-thirties. Hard to believe he'd managed to stay single for so long. "I may have left my tape measure when I was here last time."

"Wondered where that came from." He pointed to the top of a box in the far corner where the fist-size metal device rested.

"Ah ha. That's it." She stepped across the room and slipped the measuring tape into her jacket pocket. "Thanks."

Bryce clapped his hands, then rubbed them together. "So, what do you think? Just the kind of place you'd like to raise your kids?"

"Looks great. Reyna and Jason will be thrilled."

"Hope so. Took your suggestion to paint all the walls the same light color. Carpet's set for delivery next week. Same shade throughout the house."

Kara laughed. "Glad to know that there's one man in the universe who can follow directions."

Meg appeared behind him, arms laden with D-ringed fabric samples, Joe's son Davy at her side. "You were right about the paint, Kara. It makes the whole place seem bigger, doesn't it? Not so chopped up like before with different colors of paint and carpet in every room. I'm going to remember that when we fix up the second floor at our new place."

"I get my own room," Davy piped up, his dark eyes sparkling as he slipped his hand into that of his soon-to-be mom. From the look on her face, Meg loved every moment of her new life. Funny how her friend's dream had always been to live in Canyon Springs—and her own had been to be anywhere but here.

Folding muscled arms across his broad chest, Bryce's gaze settled on her. "You're heading back to the big city, are you?"

"Week after next."

"Everyone sure misses you, gal. Thought maybe you'd be stickin' around this time. You know, considering."

"Mom's illness, you mean?"

"Mmm, not exactly." His tone held a teasing note, his eyes twinkling.

"Considering what?" Meg demanded, giving him a punch in the arm. "If you've figured out a way to keep Kara in town, spill it, you big lug."

"Oh, let's just say…" Bryce chuckled, his friendly eyes still focused on her. "A reliable source saw Kara riding around town with Trey Kenton Sunday afternoon."

Her heart jerked and a wave of heat pulsed through her. Meg's pointed gaze questioned silently.

Bryce winked. "But my informant didn't report if it was a case of sittin' courtin' close. Eh, Kara?"

With a deliberate show of banging the back door, Trey stepped out of the laundry room and into the kitchen. He shouldn't have eavesdropped like that, letting a rockin' country song cover the sounds of his entry. But when he'd heard Kara's sweet voice and Bachelor Bryce flirtatiously chatting her up, he'd paused a little too long in making an entrance.

A startled Kara turned in his direction, her face flushing.

"Good afternoon, folks." He nodded a greeting to Bryce, Meg and Davy, then focused on the pretty, flustered woman.

A nervous smile played over her lips. Probably wondering what he'd overheard. It did seem that small towns had eyes and ears open at all times. That would take some getting used to. But surely she couldn't have missed the wistfulness in Bryce's tone when he asked her if she'd be leaving town. Said "everyone" missed her. Any fool could hear the disappointment in his voice at her affirmative response.

Not surprising. Any single man in his right mind would find her departure disheartening news. Why was it, though, that every time he took a shine to a woman in this town, there was always a rival hovering in the wings? Whoa. *A shine to Kara?* Naw. Just the aftershocks of a teenage crush.

"Didn't see your vehicle outside." If he had, he'd have come back later.

"I parked at the church. Ran in to retrieve my measuring tape." She pulled it from her pocket as proof. "So you're working on the parsonage, too?"

"As often as I can."

She turned to Bryce. "I need to run. Errands to finish. But it sure was good seeing you again."

"Likewise. Get yourself back home more often. Don't be such a stranger."

She said her goodbyes to Meg and Davy, then glanced uncertainly at Trey. With a stiff smile she slipped past him, heading to the door, but he caught her upper arm and brought her to a halt. Startled eyes met his and he raised an inquiring brow.

"Have a minute to spare? We have a little business to discuss."

Chapter Nine

His words sent her heart plummeting. Why, whenever she saw him, did such an excruciating combination of guilt and teenage longing twist through her? Had he heard Bryce's comment about sitting courtin' close? Maybe he'd now recognize that small towns could be invasive if you valued your privacy. She'd already warned Mom against any further "making nice" with Trey in hopes that a little romance might persuade her to stick close to town. No way would she be willing to live in this fishbowl again.

With a tip of his hat toward Bryce, Meg and Davy, Trey motioned Kara toward the laundry room door, then followed her through the garage and into the driveway. No doubt she'd get a phone call from Meg tonight, demanding to know what was up with the Sunday afternoon cruise with Cowboy.

What business did he need to discuss right now? Hadn't she made herself clear that she wouldn't help him point fingers at Canyon Springs residents?

He walked her out to the street. "I talked to your mom."

"Sounds like I'm in trouble."

He pulled gloves from his pockets. "No, no trouble. I'm accepting her offer to move in before the rental papers are signed. Will transfer my office assistant into the apartment tomorrow."

Now she'd be tripping over him until she left town.

"Your mom said you could let me in through the back of the Warehouse." His gaze remained steady, as if watching for her reaction. "Said moving in by that route is easier than the street-side staircase."

"It's quite a bit wider. Has a landing so it isn't so steep. There's a better place to pull up a truck, too."

"So tomorrow afternoon? That's good with you?"

"Sure. Let Mom know when." She thrust her hands into her jacket pockets. "I'll make sure Roxanne's there to let you in."

Was that a flicker of disappointment in his eyes?

"Thanks. Appreciate it."

"So, you're moving only your office or yourself, too?"

"Office for now. Then as soon as I get my horses settled in at their new home, I won't have to run back and forth out to Jason and Reyna's to take care of them. Can stay here in town."

She motioned toward the parsonage. "House is looking good, isn't it?"

"I'm glad the church members decided on a complete remodel. Even without the summer monsoon winds knocking a tree into the chimney and ripping up the roof, it was due for an overhaul." He shook his head. "Sixty-year-old house. You should have seen it before they gutted the place in September. Fifties' tile. Sixties' fixtures. Seventies' shag carpet and eighties' wallpaper. The appliances were so ancient, I think they came by covered wagon."

"That's right, you lived in the parsonage for a while. Does it seem strange to see it again?"

"Not quite so much now that they busted out that wall between the kitchen and dining room, added the bay window. A master bath. But at first it was like stepping back in time."

Which couldn't have been a good feeling.

She took a step into the street, then stopped. "I want to apologize for coming across so negative yesterday. About your investigation, I mean. It's just that I don't want the past hurting you even worse than it did the first time."

Surprise sparked in his intent gaze.

"You're not the first person to caution me." He kicked a booted toe at a snow clod. "Jason's put in his two cents' worth."

"You have your heart set on staying here, don't you?"

He pulled off his hat and ran a hand through his hair. "I reckon so. There's nothing I want more than to settle down in one place. Be a full-time uncle."

And eventually a full-time dad? He'd find a local girl who'd be into horses and kids and homemaking. Someone with whom he didn't share a muddled, mixed-up past. A warmhearted gal without a speck of deceit in her, who'd make up for all the post-fire years he'd endured.

Kara fisted her fingers in her pockets. The woman who'd eventually win his heart wasn't even in sight yet and already she resented her. Couldn't stand the thought of her cuddling in close to Trey. Being there for him. Encouraging him. Standing by him come what may.

Please, God, one little favor? Don't let her be anyone I know.

"I've been doing some thinking," Trey continued, oblivious of the internal hostility directed at his name-less future bride, "about what you and Jason said. And I realize I need to back off. Trust that God will open the doors He wants opened."

Was that her problem, too? That she hadn't yet waited long enough to see any good come from her father's departure? From the fire? The promise to Lindi? But look at things now—even worse than they'd ever been.

"Mom says God can work bad things out for the good." Here she was parroting words to encourage Trey that she wasn't sure she even believed. Or rather, words she believed for other people, but not herself.

His brows knit together. "I get too impatient. Sometimes it feels like the whole town knows a secret and no one's letting me in on it."

"Everybody doesn't know a secret, Trey." She could say that with certainty.

"Maybe not. But someone knows."

Two someones to be exact. She'd call Lindi tonight. Trey deserved to hear the truth.

"What do you mean you quit? I just told you I'm letting you go." Trey stared at the sixty-something woman standing in front of his secondhand wooden desk, her chubby chin jutting in obvious defiance.

What a way to start a Monday morning.

"I don't abide by lying, Marilu." He kept his tone even. Nonthreatening. "Or dishonesty of any kind."

She shook a head of gray-streaked brown curls as she rummaged in her handbag. "Never you mind that. You're the bossiest boss I've ever had and I'm not taking any more of it."

She slapped something down on the desk. His business credit card. As he watched, sensing his blood pressure rising with his every breath, she spun away to snatch her coat from the hook by the office-apartment door.

He stood. "In the business world things have to be done on the up-and-up. You have to pay your bills on time. Prove yourself trustworthy. You can't go—"

"Oh, yes, I *can* go." With a belligerent look she thrust her arms into the coat sleeves. "Watch me."

She headed out the door.

Trey maneuvered around his desk and followed her onto the landing above the stairs. "Just hold on a minute, Marilu."

"Ain't got the time, Mr. Kenton. You can mail me my check."

"About those charges—"

"Deduct 'em."

"Look, you can't walk out of here without—"

"Don't be telling me what I can and can't do, young man." She tipped her head to look at him over the top of her glasses. "I'm done with that."

She started down the stairs.

"Now hold on a minute."

"No time. Save your breath."

"But Marilu—"

"No time." She waved a dismissive hand, not pausing in her determined flight.

He watched her to the bottom of the steps, then swung around and reentered the apartment. Now what was he supposed to do? Never should have hired her in the first place, but Casey down at the gas station said she needed a job, had bookkeeping experience. That she could work from home until Trey had an office set up. He'd taken her on in early December.

After Rose quit.

You'd think with the way the economy was these days that people would appreciate a paycheck, even a part-time one. And what was she carrying on about? The bossiest boss. What did she mean by that? She'd lied right to his face. Then while arguing with him, he caught her in another lie. And another. He couldn't have any of that. Couldn't risk tainting his name, his new business. He didn't abide by lies, not even little white ones.

He returned to the desk to gaze at the clutter. Weeks ago she'd said she mailed the signed and notarized documents. The final ones that would give him the go-ahead to move his horses into the equine center property. But he'd found them on her desk Friday night, along with a paid invoice that showed *someone* had used his credit card to foot the bill for an extravagant purchase from an online cosmetics site. And a shopping channel charge. Could have been an accident the first time. Pulled out the wrong credit card or something. But twice? Did she think he wouldn't notice just because she handled the bookkeeping?

He wasn't that trusting.

Then this morning, before he'd even rolled out of bed, he'd gotten an irate call on his cell phone from the guy who was installing steel pipe fencing. The payment was a month overdue and he wouldn't show up again until the bill was paid in full.

Thank goodness he'd taken Sharon Dixon's offer to get his office set up at the Warehouse last week before the final documents were signed. Mere hours after Marilu's departure on Friday, he'd made his discoveries.

Before she showed up this morning, he'd gathered enough evidence to prove she hadn't done much of anything the past month except cruise the internet.

Had left bills unpaid. Racked up suspicious charges. Ignored unfinished documents with critical deadlines. Just what he didn't need right now. Not with a conference call with the investors scheduled for midmorning.

What he *did* need was coffee.

He glared at the little coffeemaker perched atop the filing cabinet. He'd had it for years, but the antiquated thing had given up the ghost that morning. He should have known the day would go downhill from there.

He headed to the floor-to-ceiling window to look out on the still-snowy street below. Well, he'd just have to find someone else. Sam Brooks, who ran the insurance office across the street, operated an informal job bank of sorts. Kept a bulletin board of job openings and job seekers in his entryway. He'd see who was hankerin' for office work and was willing to follow instructions. Someone who didn't cut corners and slide off into the dark side of what Marilu defensively termed "gray areas."

He called it dishonesty.

Thirty minutes later, he stomped back across the street from his visit to Sam's. Empty-handed. Nothing posted there was even close to what he needed in an office helper. He paused under the sheltering wooden porch outside the Warehouse, straightened his hat, then pulled his coat collar up around his neck to fend off the bitter wind.

Okay, he'd figure something out. He'd hand-deliver the signed permits to house his horses. And the pipe fencing payment. But first he'd call Reyna. See if she could fill in. It wouldn't be too many hours over the next few days to get those documents finalized. If she could meet the immediate deadlines, he'd have time to find permanent help.

He pulled out his cell phone and put in a quick call to his sister-in-law. But she reported that Missy had wakened complaining of a sore throat, so Reyna was a no go. The day was looking better and better.

He needed coffee. Badly.

And he knew where he could get it.

Spinning on a booted heel, he entered the toasty warm Warehouse, the little bells jingling a welcome. The gratifying aroma of fresh-brewed java met him at the door. None of that fancy flavored stuff here. Just good old-fashioned, hand-ground straight up.

He secured the door behind him, wiped his boots on the heavy-duty rug, then beelined across the hard-wood floor to the coffeemaker. Tension dissipated almost tangibly as he filled a flat-bottomed insulated cup.

"And to what do we owe the honor of your presence this early in the a.m.?" Kara's lilting voice carried from behind the checkout counter and he turned toward her.

"Mornin', Kara." He lifted the cup to her in greeting, noting how the soft green, cable-knit sweater fit her trim figure to perfection. He hadn't seen her except in passing since last week. She'd kept herself scarce. Sent Roxanne to help him with anything he needed while settling into the space upstairs.

Was she avoiding him?

He took a sip of the steaming beverage. No sugar. No cream. Just the way he liked it. "My coffeemaker croaked."

"Help yourself then. That's what it's here for."

"Thanks." He sauntered over to the counter, then something hanging off the front of it caught his eye. He reached down to unfasten the cheerful holiday reminder from its hook, then held it over his head. A cellophane-wrapped cluster of mistletoe. Red bow and all.

"Getting started early on the season, Kara?"

She groaned, then laughed and came around the counter to snatch it from his hands. "Don't you dare tell Mom you found it. She's superstitious about not getting all the Christmas stuff boxed up and put away before the new year."

"Out with the old, in with the new?"

"Exactly. Do you know how many times I've walked right by that without seeing it?" She returned to her spot behind the counter and stuffed the telltale evidence in a drawer, then put a finger to her lips. "Shh. Remember, mum's the word."

"You got it." He gripped his coffee cup, enjoying sharing a secret with Kara. Liking the way the smile lit up her face. Couldn't see that often enough to suit him. "Hey, you don't by any chance know anyone who'd like to pick up a steady paycheck doing office work, do you? Correspondence. Filing. Bookkeeping. Part-time right now, but eventually could go to forty hours—or more—when the place is up and running."

She frowned. "Don't tell me Marilu quit."

So she'd been paying enough attention to his comings and goings to know his office help's name?

"I fired her. Although she'll tell a different tale."

Kara's eyes widened. "What could that poor old thing possibly have done to get herself fired?"

"I'm not going into details." He hadn't decided if he'd press charges or let it go. Probably the latter. "But let's just say I can't abide a liar."

Kara turned away, her hand catching on a glass jar filled with stick candy, tipping it. She caught it before it rolled over the edge, then placed it back in a row with several others. Such delicate hands. Flitting like butterflies from one container to another as she straightened them.

He took a deep breath. "Can't have someone working for me that I can't trust."

"No, you can't have that." Kara focused on getting the jars arranged just right. Must be the designer in her. Looking for balance and composition.

"So did you fire Rose, too?"

He chuckled, remembering the gray-haired grandma who'd done typing for him when he'd first come to town. "Heard about Rose's departure, did you?"

She pushed one jar a half inch to the left. "And Liz."

"Now, you can't go counting Liz. Her husband got laid off and they moved out of town."

"I'm betting it would only have been a matter of time."

"Oh, you are, are you?" He cocked his head to the side and gave her an appraising look, warming to the unexpected teasing lilt to her voice. Hmm. It might be worth a shot. Maybe not smart, but what did he have to lose?

He lifted his coffee cup and took another sip, his eyes focused on her above the rim. "How are *your* typing skills, darlin'?"

Her startled gaze jerked up from the candy jars, and with a laugh she backed away faster than a ropin' horse once the loop landed 'round a running calf. "Oh, no. Not me. Get that look out of your eye."

"Just need help tomorrow. Maybe the next day or two. That's all. To tide me over until I can get a replacement. Have a deadline looming for responding to bids for arena seating. Contract prep, too. Payments need to go out. I'm up a creek without assistance."

"You've checked Sam's bulletin board?"

"Yep. And Reyna can't fill in. Missy's sick."

She frowned as she stepped back up to the counter. Gave one of the candy jars another push.

Undecided? Good sign.

"What exactly would I be doing?"

Easy boy. Don't spook her. He leaned casually against a pine support pole next to the counter and took another sip of coffee. "Entering data into the project database. Typing and proofing contracts. A little light bookkeeping. Getting everything to the post office before closing time Friday."

"That doesn't sound too involved."

"Fifteen bucks an hour." Now where'd that come from? Already giving her a hefty raise far beyond that of the other gals. But desperate times called for desperate measures, right?

She waved him off. "No pay. Roxanne says you've helped out around here this week while I've been tied up with Mom's physical therapy appointments. You've been unloading boxes. Moving shelving. Paying a vendor who was hassling her about cash on delivery. If I do it, it'd be as a favor."

If? Definitely considering it. He finished off the coffee, keeping a triumphant smile from reaching his lips. "I don't expect paybacks."

"I know you don't, but that way neither of us has to get into the tax paperwork for just a few hours employment."

"You have a point there."

"Roxanne's coming in tomorrow afternoon to give me a few hours break to run errands. But they don't have to be done right away. Just have to get them taken care of before I head back to Chicago next week."

"No pressure. I know you're busy here. I'm just a desperate man throwing out a wide loop."

"You explained why Marilu's gone. But why is it, again, that Rose departed?"

He hesitated, then came clean. "She bailed on me. Said I'm too bossy. Marilu says so, too."

Kara laughed and his heart again warmed.

"Are you? A micromanager, I mean?"

"I wouldn't go that far. But I do have standards. A quality of work I expect."

"Can't fault you for that. I'm the same way."

He waited, toying with the coffee cup, giving her time to think. Not wanting to push her. But seeing her now, eyes bright and the ponytail shimmering with her every move, doubts crept in at his impulsive bid for assistance. He'd promised himself again last night to steer clear of Kara, to keep his mind on his new project. But here he was charging in, inviting her right into the middle of his world. Not a smart move.

But she'd be working on her own most of the time. He had plenty of things to take care of elsewhere over the next few days. They'd hardly see each other.

Right?

She studied him a long moment as if similar doubts were sorting themselves out in her own mind. "Okay. I can spare a few hours. You can show me what to do in as much detail as you want to go into initially, but after that, no micromanaging."

He winked. "I promise to stay out of your hair."

And, oh, what beautiful hair.

He must be out of his mind to ask for her help.

Chapter Ten

"I can't risk it, Trey. You can't either."

Dix Dixon's gravelly voice carried clearly through Trey's cell phone.

"Telling her risks retaliation—that she'll deliberately tell someone who will tell someone and the next thing you know this promising enterprise goes down the drain because of its connection to me. And you along with it."

Trey gazed around his new Warehouse office. He didn't like this situation one bit, but he sure didn't need another strike against him, that was for sure. "It wasn't such a big deal before, but now that she's working for me—"

"She's what?"

"Yeah, I'm in a tight spot here with deadlines. Hired her to fill in when I fired Marilu yesterday. For lying. Now I feel like I'm lying by not telling Kara I'm working with you."

He'd spent an hour yesterday afternoon purging the

files, both paper and electronic, of anything having to do with her father. Hated it. Felt like deception. But he hadn't been able to get ahold of Dix until this morning.

"You're not lying. You're keeping a promise, Trey. That's all. Believe me, telling that little gal will only upset her. She hasn't said much more than two words to me since she was thirteen. If this business means anything to you, keep my involvement under your hat."

"I don't know…." Trey ran a hand through his hair. He understood Dix's predicament. Trying to make good on investments gone bad years ago. Wanting to clean up his own reputation in the community. But surely he could trust his own daughter, couldn't he?

He heard a knock at the door. Light. Possibly feminine.

"Gotta go, Dix. I think she's here."

She shouldn't have agreed to it. She should have sent Roxanne to fill in instead, even if it meant paying her triple-time. But she hadn't thought fast enough. Had given in to the onslaught of guilt that plowed into her when he'd said he'd fired Marilu.

For lying to him.

She'd almost knocked a jar of candy to the floor when he'd uttered those words. Recovered just enough to pretend to rearrange the glass canisters. Couldn't bear to look up at him.

Why'd he have to keep being so nice to her? Helping

out at the Warehouse. Even swinging by Mom's place this morning to shovel the driveway and sidewalks of a few inches of fresh snow so she wouldn't have to do it. Mom was thrilled.

Now here she sat in front of a flat-screen computer on Tuesday afternoon, typing away while Trey sat on the sofa, paperwork spread out before him on the coffee table. His afternoon meeting in Show Low had been canceled but, true to his word, he didn't micromanage. Not much anyway.

At least not once he figured out she could find her way around his word processing software and the spreadsheets and database. He'd finally settled down to review bids, Rowdy at his feet. Still seemed antsy, though. From the corner of her eye she sensed restless movement. Shifting. Heard the rustle of papers.

Knew he was looking at her. Again.

He cleared his throat. "So how are things going in the big city, Kara?"

She paused, fingers poised above the keyboard as she struggled to bring to mind Garson Design. Seven weeks she'd been gone now. It seemed fuzzy, light-years away. "Love it there. It would be perfect if I could just stay in Chicago long enough to land that promotion."

He gave a low whistle. "Promotion, huh?"

She placed her hands in her lap and turned to face him. "Not to a lead designer or anything of that magnitude. I'm still on the beginner rung. But it will be my first promotion. A step up. An increase in responsibility. Maybe in salary."

"Glad to hear they're treating you right." He scratched the late-afternoon stubble along his jaw as though deep in thought. "So you have what—like a condo or something back there?"

Her inner eye flew to the cramped, two-bedroom high-rise apartment she split with three roommates. "I'm not home that much, so I share a place with friends."

"Coworkers? Interior designers, too?"

"Actually, no. Just friends."

Sort of. She didn't intend to tell him she'd landed her living quarters through a rental agency. Other single women, total strangers, looking for someone to foot a quarter of the sky-high rent. Not exactly home sweet home, but at least it wasn't too awfully far from the design studio. Unfortunately, there had been talk of disbanding when the lease was up at the end of March, so she might soon be beating the bushes for another housing option.

"Guess I don't need to ask if your heart's still set on going back."

She smiled at him, shoving away the memory of Bryce's embarrassing comment about a possible involvement with Trey making her reconsider. "Everybody keeps asking me that, like I'm going to change my mind. But there's an energy there. A vitality. Something new and exciting always happening."

"I get the feeling you don't feel that 'energy' when you come back to Canyon Springs."

She pursed her lips in thought. How honest could she be with him? "This is a sleepy little place where everything always stays the same. Each time I enter the city limits, it's like the world grows smaller. Moves in slow motion."

"And that's a bad thing?" He leaned back on the sofa, studying her with a lazy smile. "That's why tourists come here. Pay good money for it, too."

She hooted. "Too much in my opinion."

"Maybe. But they dream about cutting their ties to the rat race and settling down in a town like this. The forest surroundings. Rustic atmosphere. Peace and quiet. The friendly faces of people who know you and call you by name."

She laughed again. "That is precisely what drives me nuts. Makes me claustrophobic. Everybody knowing me, knowing my business even before I do."

"Seems kind of reassuring to me. Like people care. You forget, I moved all over the West while growing up. New faces, new places. Never in one place long enough to call it home. Same thing on the rodeo circuit."

She studied him, stretched out on the sofa. "So you see the same thing in Canyon Springs that the seasonal visitors see?"

"I see real people. People who aren't cookie cutters of each other. People who take the time to relate on a personal level. Make an effort to get along." His smile warmed her more than it should have, and her heart gave an unexpected flutter. "Folks who are willing to help out when the occasion arises. Aren't afraid to get their hands dirty with what life deals out to them. People who aren't perfect and cut others some slack."

"Kind of idealistic, don't you think?" she teased.

"I've recently been informed by a former local," he said, his own smile tugging, "that my vision of Canyon Springs is a myth."

"But you're not buying that, are you?"

"Seems to me that most people can be about as happy as they make up their minds to be, no matter where they live."

With a shrug she maneuvered away from his pointed comment. She was happy, wasn't she? Just *happier* when she wasn't in Canyon Springs. She stood and moved to the filing cabinet. "So you're giving up rodeoing like Meg says?"

He twirled his pen with his fingers. "Didn't have a choice. Not once that bull all but pried my kneecap off on the side of a chute a year and a half ago."

She cringed. "Ouch."

"Yeah, ouch just about says it all." He chuckled and slapped his leg. "Gate was as wide open as a Kansas prairie, but he just kept ramming my leg into it again and again. So mad at having me on his back he couldn't even see the way out."

"I'm sorry." He'd fallen in love with horses, ranches and rodeo as a kid, back when his folks were filling in at a church outside Tucson. It might not be a way of life that held any attraction for her—or her mom— after her dad left, but it had meant the world to Trey. She remembered that much from their high school years. Years she'd tried in vain to push out of her memory.

His smile broadened. "But you know, it all works out. You don't see a lot of old bull and bronc riders around. So it's not like I thought rodeo was something I'd be doing until I qualified for Social Security. It was good while it lasted."

"But it has to be disappointing. To give up a dream. I know how I'd feel if I had to give up my life at Garson Design."

He held her gaze for a thoughtful moment. "I didn't like it back then, but my folks made me promise to finish college before I hit the circuit. I felt like I owed them after all they went through with me. Here in town, you know?"

How could she forget?

"Anyway," he continued, "I rodeoed on the side until I got a business degree, then full-time. Now I've come back full circle. Canyon Springs."

"Managing Duffy's place."

"When he died, his wife put the property on the market. A dozen guys who'd rodeoed with Duff back in the good old days pooled their resources with a few others to buy it. They didn't have anyone to bring it up to speed, though, until they heard I'd been put out of commission."

"So now here you are."

"Man's gotta eat." Lines crinkled around his eyes. "Besides, once I clear my name—"

That again.

"Or rather," he corrected himself, "after God clears my name—it will be pretty sweet. Settling down near family. Watching my nieces grow up."

Courting some hometown honey?

"Plan to buy property, too," he added. "You may remember I always wanted to train quarter horses."

He'd totally bought into the small-town fairy tale. As much as he hated people lying to him, why'd he keep lying to himself?

"You think this town," she warned as gently as she could, "will embrace you even if God flushes out the bad guy?"

A spark of hurt flashed through his eyes. "I'd like to think so. You don't give people here enough credit, Kara."

Why was he so willing to forgive what Canyon Springs had done to him? She sure wasn't that generous. "I guess I just have to wonder what makes a tumbleweed kind of guy think he can be happy in a place like this. My dad sure couldn't. Not even after his big talk about being a family man. What a joke."

Inwardly Kara cringed. Why'd she say that? It sounded so harsh. Bitter.

His forehead creased. "Every man isn't like your

father, Kara. And even a good man can make mistakes."

"I didn't mean to imply—"

"Knock knock." The booming, cheerful words came from the landing at the top of the stairs, accompanied by a door-rattling series of fist pounds.

Irritated at the interruption, Kara watched the knob turn, the door open and Trey's brother peep in. His gaze swept the room, then focused on her with a gleam of interested surprise. He stepped inside, a ponytailed Mary balanced on a hip and a pink backpack clutched in his free hand.

"Sorry to interrupt, bro. Didn't know you had company." His gaze lingered on her again, eyes twinkling. Jason had always been full of teasing humor, but right now wasn't a good time. Maybe he read it in her expression, for he deposited Mary on the floor and turned to Trey, motioning to the papers scattered across the coffee table. "Is that paperwork on a place you've been looking at?"

"No, not that far along yet." Trey sat up and tossed his pen to the table. "Had to let Marilu go yesterday. Kara's filling in so I can make a deadline."

Jason nodded approval in her direction, eyes dancing once again. "Well, aren't you an answered prayer?"

She forced a smile and waved a hand toward the computer. "If I can meet the deadline."

"So what can we do for you?" Trey drew his brother's attention once more.

"Could I drop off Mary for an hour? Maybe ninety minutes?" He looked hopefully from Trey to her, then back to his brother. "Reyna's got her hands full with Missy. She's definitely come down with something. Running a fever now. But I have a counseling session I can't miss."

"Reyna's mom—"

"Is still out of town. Her sisters are at work. Or nursing sick ones of their own. Wouldn't want Mary to be exposed."

Trey sat back, gazing at the paperwork. "I don't know—"

"I wouldn't ask if I had an alternative. You know that."

Trey rubbed the back of his neck. "Sure. Leave her here."

"Thanks. I—"

"Yeah, I know. You owe me. Another one. Running up quite the tab aren't you, Jas?"

"Right." Jason grinned, then crouched to help Mary out of her coat and boots. In a flash he pulled bunny-faced and cottontailed house slippers from her back-pack and snugged them onto her feet. Looked like he'd come to town kid-equipped. And if Kara wasn't mistaken, the pink T-shirt jammies she'd given Mary poked out of the bag as well. It looked as if Uncle Trey was being set up for a sleepover.

As much as he claimed he wanted to settle down in Canyon Springs, how long would it be before the charm of that wore off? Before it got old. Irritating.

Before he'd had enough of pseudo-daddy duty, saddled up and rode out of town again.

Just like her dad.

No big surprise, once her daddy was out the door Mary beelined for Kara who'd again seated herself at the computer. It was like the kid was magnetized or something. Couldn't say he blamed her. Kara was a mighty appealing woman. At times.

He watched Kara's expression soften as she turned her head so his niece could pat her silky ponytail. Listened as she oohed and aahed over Mary's beribboned hair as well. Heard Mary giggle, then watched her crawl into Kara's lap. Looked like work was on hold until Mary got her first keyboarding lesson.

"Mary. M-A-R-Y," Kara's sweet, soft voice spelled out for the youngster as she guided a little finger to each letter.

He ran a hand through his hair. So Kara didn't think the townspeople would find it in their hearts to accept him even if he proved his innocence.

"Missy. M-I-S-S-Y."

But wasn't it more likely that they'd be grateful? More than happy to have a bad apple weeded out, to welcome another solid citizen into the community?

"Kara. K-A-R-A."

He wasn't buying her pessimistic take on it. No doubt in his mind God had brought him back to town. Even if God was taking his own sweet time about it, he was here to resolve unfinished business, to prove himself innocent of wrongdoing. What other reason could there be?

He studied the gentle curve of Kara's cheek. The silken swing of her red-gold hair caught up in a sea-green satin ribbon. The soft, smiling bow of her lips… He swallowed, remembering how sweet they'd tasted that night long ago.

No, he didn't fear the community's reaction when he cleared his name. Not even if the culprit was the mayor himself. They'd come around. Eventually. No, it was the other thing she'd said that gut-kicked him. When she spoke the word that still rang in his ears. That exposed his insecurity. Voiced his secret doubts.

Tumbleweed.

She'd without reservation pegged him as a drifter. A transient. A rolling stone. Didn't believe him inherently capable of putting down roots. Was openly skeptical that he could make a commitment to a community.

And to a woman as well?

Was her thinking all tangled up because of her folks' divorce? Or could the thing he most feared about himself be true? Was blatantly clear to others?

"Trey. T-R-E-Y."

His ears barely registered the feminine voices. Maybe Kara was right. His ex-girlfriend had said the same thing. T-U-M-B-L-E-W-E-E-D.

A laughing Mary spun in Kara's lap and pointed at him. "That's you, Uncle Trey!"

Chapter Eleven

"Will you come to my Valemtime's Day party, Kara?"

She didn't correct Mary's sweet mispronunciation of the holiday. As she'd predicted, the little girl stayed the previous night with Trey. He'd told his niece this morning that Kara was working and not to bother her. But now, with her uncle dashing out to his truck to retrieve more paperwork, the little girl wasted no time crawling into her lap.

"Thank you for inviting me, sweetheart, but I'm going back to Chicago next week."

"But you gotta come."

"I wish I could."

"Daddy kissed Mommy on Valemtime's Day when they were in high school."

"He did?"

"Uh-huh. They were sixteen. Then they got married. How old are you, Kara?"

"Twenty-eight."

Mary's forehead puckered, then she nodded as if coming to a conclusion. "Me and Missy want Uncle Trey to stay in Canyon Springs. If you kiss him, he'll stay."

Oh, my. Memory flew to the one time she *had* kissed him. Thoroughly.

"Mommy says he needs to kiss a girl and get married and stay here."

How to respond to that? "I imagine there are lots of girls in this town who would like to kiss—and marry—your uncle."

"But I want you."

"I'm afraid I live a long, long way from here. In a big city. I'm just visiting my mom while she's sick."

"But if you kiss Uncle Trey you can live here, too." Her dark eyes emphasized the sincere appeal. "You won't have to be so far away from me and Missy."

"Sweetie, I—"

At the sound of heavy footsteps on the landing outside the door, Mary's eyes widened and she scrambled off Kara's lap. Dashed across the room and threw herself on the sofa.

Just as Trey entered the apartment, the phone vibrated in the purse nestled at Kara's feet. She snatched it up, hoping Lindi was returning her persistent calls. They could set a time to meet in private.

But the caller ID wasn't Lindi's.

"You are aware, aren't you, Kara, that I'm holding this position open for you?" The voice of Spencer Alexander III of Garson Design echoed through the receiver. Her heartbeat accelerated and she glanced at Trey as he and Mary, hand in hand, headed to the kitchen.

"Gabrielle won't wait much longer," her boss continued, and she pictured his aristocratic countenance indulging in a frown. "She's afraid with the economic uncertainty that the board will nix the upgraded position altogether."

"I'm sorry, Spence. I had no idea when I left Chicago that my mother was as bad off as she was. But she's on the road to recovery, and I have my flight booked for next Monday."

"Excellent. You've been working on the NuTowne project, I assume? I told Gabrielle you were."

"Every spare minute." Minutes that only materialized after a late dinner and into the wee hours of the morning. Thank goodness for design software and the ability to log into the company system remotely. And for caffeine.

"Excellent. That will work in your favor."

"I appreciate all you're doing for me." She tightened her grip on the phone, knowing how much it meant to have a designer of Spence's caliber in her corner. "Once I get back, I'll make it up to you. I promise."

She glanced toward the kitchen from where Mary's childish voice scolded Trey for inadequate jelly on her peanut butter sandwich. Caught herself smiling at his indignant, rumbling response peppered with good ol' boy cowboy jargon he exaggerated to make his niece laugh.

"Kara?" Spence's voice drew her back to their conversation. "Text me your flight info and I'll pick you up at O'Hare."

She agreed, then with a smile returned the phone to her purse. The promotion was hers. And not even a frowning Trey, now watching from where he leaned against the wooden door frame of the kitchen, could steal away the tingle of anticipation.

"Looks like a lot of work to me." Trey flipped through a few more pages of the spiral-bound workbook. Then he tossed it back on his brother's desk. A premarital counseling workbook. One like Meg and Joe would be completing in the coming weeks.

He nudged a stack of related videos. "I mean, if it's right, if God's in it, why all the boot camp stuff? If it takes all this not to end up in a divorce court, maybe people should be rethinking the whole shootin' match."

Which is what his once-upon-a-time girlfriend, Tanya Tyber, had done three years ago. Hit the door running when after twenty-two months and fifteen days—yep, she had it figured down to the days—he still hadn't put a ring on her finger.

"That's why we do this." Jason tapped the workbook cover. "Separates the goats from the sheep, so to speak. Or at least alerts the starry-eyed to the realities of wedded bliss."

Even after all this time the memory of Tanya's departure left him shaken. Her words still wounded.

Scarred. He'd heard them echoed, in more gentle tones, in Kara's evaluation of him yesterday. But Tanya had believed him incapable of settling down. Keeping a commitment.

The very thing he, too, feared.

"I only wish more would take time to build a stronger foundation," his brother continued. "Everyone's in such a rush. Afraid if they don't tie the knot and tie it fast, their life's ruined. If only they knew the half of it—what ruin looks and feels like once you're in the middle of a bad marriage."

Trey picked up the doll he'd come to retrieve for his niece, having left Mary in Kara's company. "Don't kid yourself, Jas, it's not easy being single, finding someone who shares your values. Your beliefs. Hard enough without others judging you."

"Easier than being unhappily married."

Trey snorted. "Won't argue with that, but there are people—even church people—who make sure you know you're not up to their standards if you don't have that ring on your finger. Or a certificate of divorce in hand to show that you at least 'qualified' at one point in time."

"You don't mean people like Reyna, do you?"

He frowned. Where'd he get an idea like that? His brother was as dense as a rock sometimes. "No, not Reyna. She wants me to be happy. To settle down near the girls."

He moved to the open office door, then swung around again to face his brother. "No, I mean the ones who disregard that it's either not God's timing or not his best plan. Insinuate there's something inherently wrong with you."

Jason pushed back in his chair, donning his irritatingly benign, pastor-like countenance. "I'm sensing dormant hostility here. Residual Tanya? If you want to talk about it, I have a cancellation on my schedule at—"

"Sense whatever you want to, Jas. I'm done talking. I've got to get back to work."

Pulling the office door closed behind him, Trey exited the building by the back door. Now why'd he have to go getting irritated like that? Jas meant well. It wasn't his fault women didn't trust his older brother.

He pulled up his jacket collar against the buffeting wind, then headed for his truck. His heart felt pounds heavier than it had a few days ago. He shouldn't have asked Kara to help out. Handed her the opportunity to voice her opinion of his Canyon Springs dream. To label him a drifter. Forced him to overhear her talking sweet to some big-city hotshot she worked with.

At least they'd made the deadline with room to spare. She'd get back to her own business at the Warehouse now and he'd look for other office help. But why, of all things, did he have to go thinking about Tanya for the second day in a row?

And why was he foolish enough to think he could somehow prove to the pretty Miss Dixon that she was wrong about him?

* * *

Late Friday afternoon Kara pulled out a drawer on her mom's home office desk, searching for a stamp. But her mind wasn't on dropping a postcard to her Aunt Tammy.

Lindi still wasn't answering her phone or responding to text messages. Nor had she been in when Kara stopped by her office. Out on catering business she'd been told. So what was stopping her from telling Trey? Nothing. Right this minute she could barge into his office and get it over with. But she'd already ruined Trey's life—now it fell to her to ruin Lindi's as well?

She pulled open another drawer. Where were those stamps? They used to be in that wooden, decoupaged box. The one she'd made in grade school for Mom's birthday. She shut the drawer and tried another. No luck. The next drawer stuck for a moment, then slid out. Empty, except for an eight-by-ten photo frame facedown at the bottom. Curious, she turned it over.

The room dimmed as a cloud obliterated the sun that only moments before had beamed through the western-facing window. Kara stared down at the photograph. There they were. The happy family. Or at least the ten-year-old decked out in cowgirl gear had thought they were. Seated on the fence rail between her parents, she looked close to bursting with it, grinning from ear to ear.

Eighteen years ago. Just three years before Dad hit the road. Three years wasn't a very long time.

People didn't just wake up some morning and decide to betray the trust of those around them, did they? Pull up stakes? Had he already been floundering financially? Scrambling to make good on the investments entrusted to him by friends? Restless. Impatient. Ready to move on even as he stood there smiling for the photographer, his arm wrapped around his daughter's waist.

Her grip tightened on the frame. Had Mom sensed he wasn't a home-and-hearth kind of man? That one day he'd leave her behind? How years of hard work on his behalf would mean she'd never find a way back to her own dream? A dream of teaching kindergarten that Aunt Tammy once confided she'd had since childhood.

She flipped the frame over and closed it in the drawer again. She hoped he was proud of himself. Him and his second family over there in New Mexico.

Now where was that stamp box?

She pulled open the remaining drawer. Ah, there it was, peeping out from under a stack of haphazardly crammed, overflowing manila file folders. She lifted out the fat wedge of folders and retrieved the stamp box with her free hand. But the smooth surfaces of the stack slid against each other and one dropped to the floor, scattering papers.

Setting aside the little box and folders, she then knelt to clean up the mess. Looked to be business stuff. Invoices and bills. Receipts. She scooped them up, straightening them to be returned to the folder, when one caught her eye.

OVERDUE.

Stamped in red block letters on the face of the bill. She didn't mean to snoop, but couldn't help but take a closer look. She shuffled through the other documents. Insurance papers. Medical bills. Invoices for Warehouse inventory.

Overdue. Final Notice.

Tons of them. What was going on? With a sense of uneasiness, she scooped them into the folder and headed to the kitchen where her mother sat sewing a button on a shirtsleeve.

"Mom, what's this all about?"

Her mother looked up with a smile. "What's what all about, doll?"

Kara placed the overflowing file folder in front of her. At the look on Mom's face, her heart stumbled.

"What were you doing in my things?"

"Looking for stamps."

Mom set aside the sewing, then pulled the manila folder toward her. "Guess you found more than you bargained for, didn't you?"

"What's going on, Mom?" Her mother's flat, unemotional response scared her more than the bills. The weariness, the resignation, in her tone. "There's all sorts of stuff here. Late payment notices. Letters saying you're going to be turned over to a collection agency."

Mom frowned. "It's mostly a cash flow problem.

You know, when insurance hasn't paid yet but everyone wants their share up front."

"Cash flow? Mom, there are dozens of letters asking you for payment. And it looks like you were late on the mortgage for the Warehouse the last several months, too."

"Late, but it got paid. Everything will get straightened out. Don't go getting worked up over this."

"Are you kidding?" Weak-kneed, she dropped into the chair across from Mom. "You're being threatened with legal action. And what about these overdue bills for the Warehouse? I guess this explains why the delivery guy refused to leave that shipment. Roxanne said Trey had to pay him cash or he wouldn't leave it. How can we stay in business if we don't pay our bills?"

"It will all work out."

Kara gripped the edge of the table to still her shaking hands. "Why didn't you tell me? I could have sent you money."

"Honey, I didn't see any point in worrying you about it. I know how much the job and promotion mean to you. You bought that new car. May be looking for your own apartment. You're working hard and I didn't want this to be a distraction."

Kara slumped back in the chair, anger building. How could God have let things get so out of hand?

"It's more than a distraction now."

"I'm aware of that, Kara," her mother said quietly.

"I'm working with the hospital and the doctors to see if I can pay it off gradually. It will all work out."

"You keep saying that, but these medical bills are huge. You could lose everything. Your house. The Warehouse."

"I won't lose the house. I've got my business to fall back on—and if I need to sell it to keep my home, so be it."

An invisible fist punched Kara in the midsection. Sell the Warehouse? Had her mother gone insane? "Did you think you could sell it and I wouldn't notice?"

"I don't intend to file for bankruptcy, if that's what you're thinking. I pay my debts."

Kara smacked the table with the flat of her hand. "No way are you going to lose the Warehouse, Mom. You almost lost it when Dad left us and you worked your tail off to keep it. I'm going back to Chicago. If I have to, I'll live out of my car. I'll get a second job—selling hot dogs on a street corner if that's what it takes. You are not losing the Warehouse."

Mom rose to her feet, then braced her hands on the back of her chair. "This is exactly why I didn't tell you. It may be that this is all for the best. The Warehouse has gotten to be a handful in recent years. Maybe it's time to let it go. Retire."

Kara scoffed. "You're not old enough to retire."

"Then maybe I need a desk job. Regular hours. I've been at the Warehouse since before you were born.

That's a long time, honey. Someone will be willing to take it off my hands."

Kara's breath caught. "Does anyone else know about the bills? I mean, Mom, if it comes to selling the Warehouse and people know you *have* to sell or go into foreclosure, they're going to make a low offer. Super-low. Please tell me this isn't common knowledge and that I'm the last to find out."

Mom pulled the chair out and again sat down. "I've never been one to broadcast my personal affairs and you know it. I'd intended to cancel that standing order, the one Trey probably had to pay cash for. It slipped my mind. But I make sure local vendors get paid on time."

Kara let out a gust of pent-up breath. "Good, good. That gives me some time. I can—"

Mom laid her hand over Kara's. "Honey, just relax. Everything's going to be fine. I'll pay my bills one way or another and if that means letting the Warehouse go—making a change in lifestyle—well, if that's what the good Lord wants, I'll do whatever is necessary."

Kara pulled her hands free and staggered to her feet, almost knocking over the chair. "Quite frankly, Mom, I don't care what the good Lord wants. I'm telling you right now, you're not going to lose the Warehouse. I won't allow it."

Chapter Twelve

By the time he'd gotten his horses tended to and headed into town on Saturday morning to complete much-needed manual labor at the horse facility, Trey had a hankerin' for a cup of coffee. Warehouse coffee.

The door jingled its usual welcome as he entered, but he didn't make it to the coffeemaker before Kara came out from the back of the store. He halted and, without even thinking, gave a low whistle. "Whoa. Look at you."

Kara's face pinked as she self-consciously glanced down at her just-above-the-knee skirt and fitted, sage-green jacket. High, strappy heels. That may be standard business attire in Chicago, but oh, man, did she stand out in the casual capitol of the world, Canyon Springs.

He couldn't take his eyes off her. The way she'd looped her hair on top of her head. The glint of gold studs in her ears. The fine chain at her throat.

He caught a whiff of faint, woodsy perfume as she slipped past him to the checkout counter, her spiky heels tapping on the wooden floor as she avoided his gaze. His heart beat a little faster.

"So what's the occasion?"

"I'm running to Show Low this morning just as soon as Roxanne gets in." She glanced at him. "Business. That meet with your approval, Cowboy?"

Anything having to do with Kara this morning would meet with his approval. Looked like it was going to be his lucky day. "I'm headed that way myself. Care to ride along?"

"I—" Alarm flickered in her gaze, and he glanced down at his hay-matted jacket, worn jeans and scuffed boots. *Good goin' there, Kenton.* Like a woman dressed like *that* would want to be seen with someone who looked like they'd just walked out of a barnyard. Which was exactly where he'd been.

He scrubbed a hand across his jaw. Forgot to shave again, too. Doggone it. He mustered a wink. "I take that as a no?"

Her sweet as honey-butter-on-a-biscuit smile surfaced. "Thanks for offering, but I need my own transportation today."

"Offer stands anytime. I head over that way about once a week." He grinned. "Generally clean up before I go."

"Thanks, but I'm leaving town on Monday."

"Right." Like he could forget.

She hugged her arms to herself and moved away

from him, the floor creaking under her dainty feet. She looked around the rustic expanse as if seeing it for the first time. Beamed ceiling. Earth-toned Navajo rugs hanging on the walls above the merchandise. The faint scent of wood smoke and coffee. Early morning sunlight pouring in the windows to dapple the worn, planked flooring.

"You can't believe all the memories I have of this place." She turned to him with a wistful smile. "Bet you didn't know this is where I took my first steps."

He couldn't help returning her smile, picturing her as she must have been as a toddler. Sounded like she was gearing up mentally for her Chicago departure. Feeling nostalgic. "And I'm betting those feet were running straight out the door, right? Couldn't get out of here fast enough."

"Believe it or not, at one time my biggest dream was to grow up and run the Warehouse myself."

He arched a disbelieving brow. "How old were you? Three?"

"Actually, it was something I wanted to do for a long time. Until I turned thirteen."

Up until the time her dad walked out.

She again gazed around the room. "I had all these ideas, you know? Beginner designer-type ideas, I guess. For seasonal displays. Dressing up the windows. A cozy seating arrangement near the woodstove. Reading lamps. A lending-library shelf."

"Sounds homey." He studied her, seeing a side of Kara he hadn't seen since his return.

"As a kid I was the original Wrangler girl. Designer duds?" She motioned to her outfit. "Who cared? Give me my horse and a free Saturday afternoon and I'd be happy."

"You had a horse?"

His expression must have reflected his shock because she laughed. "You think the daughter of a rodeo cowboy wouldn't?"

"I never heard you talk about horses when we were in high school. You never hung out at Duffy's with me." Had he just not been paying attention?

"Cinnabar. Red roan. Registered American quarter horse. The fastest little barrel racer you ever saw."

How had he missed this? "You? A barrel racer?"

Kara laughed. "Rodeo Queen Sharon Dixon wouldn't stand for anything less."

"You're kidding. Sharon?" The image of her mother negotiating her way around a tri-barreled arena on a walker flashed through his mind.

"How do you think she met Dad?" Kara's eyes danced, clearly amused at his reaction to her revelation.

He bumped up the rim of his hat with a knuckle. "Guess I never thought about it. How'd they end up here?"

She shrugged. "They met on the rodeo circuit. Got married. Eventually got pregnant and decided to settle down in the town Mom grew up in. Where she'd inherited her father's business. Renamed it for my dad. And the rest is history."

Now if this just didn't beat all. He stared at Kara as if seeing her for the first time.

"You look like you just got lobbed off a bull." Her teasing laugh echoed in his ears. "And hit the ground pretty hard."

He chuckled. "I'm still trying to get my head around you being a horsewoman. And Sharon, too."

"By the time I met you, Cinnabar was long gone. I didn't talk about him. Didn't want anything to do with horses. It hurt too much. I think it killed Mom as much as it did me when we had to get rid of them after Dad left. He took his, of course." Her expression hardened. "But she couldn't afford to keep ours."

He frowned. Why couldn't Dix have made sure this little gal kept her horse instead of sticking her with an old Ford Mustang she never drove? Maybe he didn't know him quite as well as he thought he did.

"We didn't have time to ride or care for them anyway," Kara continued. "Had to make up for the hours Dad vacated at the Warehouse. It was a huge responsibility for Mom to keep this place going by herself. Came close to losing it."

She turned away, her hand trailing along a rack of jackets.

He remembered the little free time Kara had as a teen. How he'd wanted to spend more time with her, but she'd beg off. Her mom always needed her at the Warehouse. He'd figured it was her mother's way of keeping him at a safe distance. But maybe not.

"Losing your horse, that must have been a blow."

He knew how attached you got to those big hairy critters.

She turned again to him, her gaze softening with a wistfulness that tugged at his heart. "I loved that horse."

His jaw tightened. He hated seeing her like this. Sad over something that happened when she'd been a kid. If he could get his hands around Dix's throat right now… Guilt pierced his conscience. She'd get her hands around *his* throat if she found out he was keeping his connection to her father a secret. He had to get ahold of Dix. Talk him into letting him tell her.

"Would you like to go riding? I'll be moving my horses to the new facility tomorrow. Big indoor arena."

He'd never thought to ask her before. Didn't know she'd ever been into horses. The Kara he first met had been, well, sort of prissy. But in a nice way. Refined. Polished. Never would have guessed she'd groomed a sweaty horse, mucked out a stall or hauled hay. The contrast intrigued him.

"I don't—"

"It's hard to keep two once-active horses exercised by myself. Especially in the winter." He gave her an encouraging nod. "They're getting mighty fat and sassy."

She shook her head, her eyes reflecting regret. "Thanks, but I'd probably fall on my fanny. It's been too long. And don't go telling me it's like riding a bike."

He chuckled. "I'm guessing it's something like that. So what do you say? Think you can set aside your citified self long enough to give old Taco or Beamer a good work out?"

"Taco and Beamer? What kind of names are those for a horse?"

"You should know registered names are a mile long. Nicknames stick. So what do you say? Want to go riding Sunday afternoon?"

A smile tugged. "I don't know...."

Sounded like she was tempted. He raised an encouraging brow. "You'd be doing me a favor. Think about it. Then let me know."

She nodded, but the little-lost-girl look still lingered. If he could just pull her into his arms. Hold her until that forlorn expression hightailed it off into the sunset. But that would be a mistake. Or rather another mistake. He was supposed to be guarding his heart. Now here he'd gone and invited her to ride with him just because he didn't like to see her sad.

Coming back to his senses, he tipped his hat in her direction. "Guess I'd best get on the road. Need to haul my horses over to Show Low to get reshod. And see a guy who has a lead on a reliable hay supplier. Lots to do today."

"Me, too."

They exchanged parting smiles, and he headed toward the door. With any luck, she'd forget he'd made the offer to go riding. She hadn't jumped at it, so probably thought being around horses would bring back too many unpleasant memories. Which was just as well because he could hardly take back the invitation now. But he'd learned his lesson. Again. Why couldn't he keep his tongue tied down? Lips always flappin' before thinking things through.

He'd just stepped out on the wooden porch, fixing to pull the Warehouse door closed, when he heard her quick high-heeled steps on the hardwood floor behind him.

"Trey?"

Hand still on the doorknob, he turned to look full in her beautiful face. At those breathlessly parted lips. The bristly-lashed gray eyes wide with uncertainty. And hope.

He swallowed. "Yeah?"

"I'll ride with you."

It was nine-thirty when she pulled into the parking lot of a bank in Show Low. Drove around to the far side where her mom's vehicle couldn't be seen from the highway, just in case Trey or another Canyon Springs local was out and about on a Saturday shopping spree in the "big city." She hadn't wanted to do business with the lone Canyon Springs bank. Didn't want to risk raising curiosity or a slip of the tongue on the part of a well-intentioned—or maybe not so well-intentioned—bank employee.

Approaching the doors of the establishment, she

caught herself saying a prayer for success, for a savvy, accommodating banker and a quick in and out and on her way. Unfortunately, forty minutes later she climbed back in the SUV. Empty-handed. Most of the time had been spent waiting for a loan rep, but she'd hardly started the paperwork before the word "collateral" popped up. It went downhill from there.

All she wanted was a personal loan to get the bills off her mother's back. Then, from Chicago, she'd pay off the loan and accrued interest. But the amount she needed went beyond a car loan. And she didn't own any property except her vehicle, which wasn't paid for. Combine that with the bottom dropping out of the economy and the bank was cautious to the extreme.

She squared her shoulders. Okay, next stop.

By one o'clock she'd made the rounds of Show Low's banking establishments without success. Would she have any better luck in Flagstaff? Phoenix? Weren't banks supposed to loan money? Isn't that how they earned their income, off the interest?

Mom said she was in negotiations to allow her to pay off the bills little by little. But gradually still meant taking away from the Warehouse. Reducing stock. Putting off upgrades and repairs. So many things made sense now that she knew the truth. The leaky roof that hadn't been fixed. The minor plumbing problem that became a major repair job in December. Patching, not replacing, a cracked window. Turning down the heat at the house. Renting the Warehouse apartment to Trey.

Had she been paying attention at all, she'd have caught the signs last spring when she'd been here. But no, she was so focused on getting back to Chicago that she didn't look beyond the surface.

So what now?

Returning to Chicago on Monday still seemed her best bet. Maybe she could secure a personal loan there. At least could start pumping funds homeward as fast as she could. But what if Mom lost the Warehouse? She'd never forgive herself if that happened. It had come way too close to that when Kara was a teen.

When she walked to the back door of her mother's house late that afternoon, she paused. Heavy cloud cover had moved in since morning, suggesting another snow system on the horizon. Through the kitchen window she could see Mom moving around in the glow of the interior light. Her hardworking mother. Who'd sacrificed so much for so long. Who always remained cheerful, encouraging, faithful. Did she have any idea how serious this latest situation was?

Kara glanced up at the steel-gray heavens. *Please, God, help me to help her.*

"Now, don't you look nice," Mom said as Kara stepped inside and peeled out of her coat. "Where've you been all dressed up like that, doll?"

She'd slipped out that morning, while her mom was in the shower. "Show Low."

Mom frowned, her gaze questioning.

"Well, someone has to do something, don't they?" Kara heard the defensiveness in her tone. "I told you I'm not going to let you lose the Warehouse."

Her mother's shoulders slumped. "So you got a loan?"

"No." Failure weighed heavily as she tossed her coat over the back of a chair. "The banks are being stingy. But I'll take care of everything as soon as I get back to Chicago."

Her mom moved to the kitchen sink to rinse out a pan, then reached for a dish towel. "You're mad at me, aren't you?"

"No. Disappointed would be a better word." She gripped the back of the chair, searching for the right words that would make her mother understand. "Why didn't you tell me so we could have handled this together? I'm not a kid anymore, Mom."

Mom turned to her, eyes filled with regret. "Oh, honey, I know you're not."

"Well then?"

"It happened so fast. Got away from me." She twisted the dish towel in her hands. "Last spring after that health setback I reduced expenditures. But when the economic bubble burst, when seasonal visitors dropped off, that's when this latest hospitalization hit. I couldn't have foreseen it. I didn't have any idea…."

Kara longed to open her arms. To pull her mother close. To tell her how much she loved her and that she'd make everything right again if it took her last dying breath. But she hesitated, not wanting to interrupt.

"Fortunately, your dad heard about the heart attack. Sent me a check to cover the Warehouse mortgage."

"What?" A roaring filled her ears as bewilderment and outrage slammed into her. "He did *what?"*

"He does that every once in a while."

"Are you kidding me? How can you think of taking anything from him? We don't need him. Never have."

"He couldn't pay much in the way of child support when you were younger, doll. But he pitched in as best he could. When he could. Always has."

"I'm just now finding out about this? That we're beholden to a man who dumped us?"

"I tried to tell you once, years ago, but you wouldn't hear me out."

Kara jerked her coat from the back of the chair. "From now on, you're not taking another dime from him. Not a penny. Not even if I have to hold down *ten* jobs."

"Kara—"

Kara raised a hand to halt her. Fought back tears.

"You know, Mom, I don't feel like discussing this anymore." She thrust her arms into the coat sleeves. "I'm going out for a while. Don't count on me for supper."

She hastily left the house, shutting the back door

harder than she intended. Heard the glass pane rattle in its wooden frame.

How could Mom have let Dad back into their lives?

Chapter Thirteen

What had she gotten herself into?

Looking down at Trey from the chestnut Taco's sturdy back, her stomach churned. Not only due to being on a horse again, but to spending personal time with Trey. It was her own fault. Talking about Cinnabar had made him feel sorry for her. Made him think he needed to *do* something.

He wouldn't feel so compassionate if he knew how she'd treated Mom last night. Tension in her arms increased, and Taco's ears twitched uncertainly until she relaxed her fingers on the reins. How had she not known Dad had been pitching in to help make ends meet? And how could Mom take money from him?

She shouldn't have lost her temper. But on top of finding out Mom's health setback was more serious than she'd let on, discovering she'd kept her dire finances secret and now learning Dad wasn't quite the bad guy she'd always believed him…well, it was too much all at once. And she'd lashed out.

Mom probably felt as bad about their falling out as she did. Things had been good between them since her most recent return. They'd grown closer. Formed a stronger bond. Enjoyed each other's company. That is, until now.

She repositioned herself in the saddle, the sound of creaking leather soothing her ruffled emotions. They'd steered clear of each other this morning. Peggy picked Mom up for church. She herself had sat with Meg and Davy. But tonight they'd have a long talk while she packed for her return to Chicago. Get everything worked out between them.

Trey thrust his fingers under Taco's saddle cinch to ensure she'd gotten it tight enough. Surprised that she had, if the raised brow was an indicator. She'd insisted on saddling up by herself. A little rusty, with fumbling fingers, but there was no point in being more of a nuisance than she already was.

He scratched Taco behind an ear, then fiddled with the headstall. The chin strap. "Looks like you're good to go."

"Feels strange to be on a horse again." She adjusted her feet in the stirrups, thankful Reyna had a pair of same-size boots to loan. "Fifteen years is a long time."

He smiled up at her. "You might surprise yourself."

"Not holding my breath."

"So, ready to roll?"

She nodded. And with a nudge of her booted heels,

she signaled the horse forward, alongside Trey, who led Beamer. Down the wide stable aisle toward an indoor arena gate, the horses' shod hooves rang hollowly on the floor. Like a kid in a candy shop, Kara filled her lungs with the familiar scent of horses, hay and leather. Happy smells from childhood.

Before Dad left.

Coming up the drive to the equine center earlier, seated next to Trey in his pickup, she'd avoided looking at the snowy, burned-out acreage. But once inside the newly remodeled space all thoughts of the fire dissipated. Her spirits rose further as Trey opened the gate to the arena and stepped back to let her pass through.

She nudged Trey's horse into the well-groomed arena, then halted, marveling at the arched roof above her head. The vastness of the open space. Taco's ears flicked back and forth, alert to the unfamiliar presence on his back, anticipating further instructions.

She glanced back at Trey who'd again shut the gate and was leaning on it with a booted toe hooked in one of its pipe slats, his folded forearms looped through Beamer's reins and resting on top. He tipped his hat to her and smiled. Guess he didn't plan to join her right off. Wanted her to get a feel for her mount and the space without distractions.

Signaling to Taco, she walked the horse around the perimeter of the arena as she shifted in the saddle, tried to find a comfortable sweet spot. Again tested out the length of her stirrups. Adjusted her reins.

Attempted to settle into a world she'd long been away from. Too long.

Although it was the same arena in which she'd worked out Cinnabar when she was a kid and spent time in with her folks, the skylights, the lighting and the other upgrades gave her a sense of being far from Canyon Springs. Far from the past.

She leaned forward to pat Taco on the shoulder. Spoke soothing, conversational words, amused at how his winter-fuzzed ears flicked back and forth to catch her every utterance.

A walk. A trot. A few times around the arena. Then she brought the gelding to a halt on the far side. Signaled him to back up. Straight line. No fuss. Then moved forward again. So far so good. Maybe it *was* like riding a bike?

Might as well find out.

"Let's see what you've got, mister." She signaled the horse into a gentle lope for a few rounds, then into a wide-open figure eight in the center of the arena.

Her scalp tingled and the sensation spread through her face, down her neck, into her arms. Oh, man, did this horse have a rocking chair gait, flawlessly changing leads as she lightly neck-reined him into a reverse. Push-button perfect.

A respect for Trey's training skills soared as she took the animal through a series of warm-ups, then back to the perimeter of the arena for a full gallop. Ponytail flying behind her, cool air brushing her cheeks, the tingling sensation coursed through each fiber of her body—and deep into her very soul.

Tears pricked her eyes.

Thank you, God. I'm flying without wings!

She'd forgotten him. So totally into the moment that she'd forgotten him.

Trey stood grinning from where he'd remained with Beamer just outside the arena. Amazing. Fifteen years and her basic skills were still intact. Instinctive. Sure, a bit rusty, but that would smooth out with time. Practice. A curious pride and sense of satisfaction welled as his trainer's eye expertly evaluated her impromptu performance.

For the first twenty minutes after she'd entered the arena, he'd noted her trying to get her bearings. Calming down. Connecting with Taco. But was she ever into it now. Ponytail sailing, settling in to the once-familiar rhythms. Taco was settling in, too, responding to her every signal. As each minute ticked by, she transformed before his eyes. From the way her left hand held the reins and her right hand, no longer clenched, rested at her thigh, he could tell she'd relaxed.

A beautiful woman on a beautiful horse.

A sight to behold.

God sure had put together a fine-looking package when he created Kara Dixon. A good-hearted woman, too, putting her dream job on hold to look out for her mom. Helping Reyna with the parsonage. Him with his deadlines. Meg and the other townspeople he encountered thought the world of her as well.

But how did a man keep from falling in love with her? How did you stop yourself from caring? Involving yourself? It could be done, because he didn't fall in love with his friends' wives or girlfriends. If only Kara had come back to town married. Or at least engaged. It would have been much easier.

Wouldn't it?

Why'd God have to go bringing her back to Canyon Springs? And to add salt to the wound she loved horses every bit as much as he did. There had to be more to it than God deciding he needed a refresher lesson in obedience. But the way things were looking, that's what it was coming down to. She stuck to her belief in a "hands-off" God. Still had the bit in her teeth, determined to shake off the dust of Canyon Springs. Leaving tomorrow.

Hold me steady, Lord.

With one last figure eight, Kara brought Taco back to a walk and headed toward Trey, unable to hide a beaming smile.

She reined in, eyes sparkling as she leaned forward to pat Taco on the neck.

"Do I ever love this horse." Laughing, she wiped at her eyes with the cuff of her jacket sleeve.

Had she been crying? A sharp pain gored him. "He's a good old boy, that's for certain."

"You trained him, right?"

"Since he first stood on wobbly legs."

"You are amazing. It was like, like—"

"Magic?"

"Yes!"

His heart swelled at her praise. If this kept up, he'd soon be buying shirts a couple of sizes larger. "Helps to have a rider on him who knows the ropes. A horse senses that. Didn't take you long to get comfortable and he responded."

"I'm still so awkward." She patted the horse again. "Poor Taco. You probably wonder why Trey's punishing you, don't you?"

"I don't hear him complaining."

Her eyes smiled into his. Radiant. Open. Vulnerable. He took a deep breath and turned to his own horse. "So what do you say we work them both out for a while?"

Preferably her on one end of the arena and him on the other.

"I'd love to. Oh, just a sec." Still smiling, she fished under the waist of her jacket. "My phone's vibrating."

He looped the reins over Beamer's head, trying not to frown. She'd carried her cell phone with her? Probably expecting a call from that Chicago guy. Spence.

Kara smiled an apology as she answered. "Hi, Meg. Out riding a horse, can you believe it?"

Her smile melted. "When? Where is she now?"

Kara's frightened eyes sought his.

"What?" he mouthed, but she shook her head. He unlatched the gate and led Beamer into the arena.

"Is she going to be okay? All right. I'm on my way."

She turned off her phone and sat stone-like, staring at him. Tried to speak, but tears choked her off.

He dropped Beamer's reins and reached up to her. She kicked her feet out of the stirrups and slung her right leg over the saddle horn. Leaned forward to slip her arms around his neck, then slid down into his arms.

"Trey."

"What is it? What happened?" he whispered, holding her trembling body in his arms. The strong, confident horsewoman suddenly so fragile.

"It's—it's Mom." Her grip tightened on his arms as she pulled slightly back and gazed into his eyes. "Meg says they think she's had another heart attack."

In a waiting room of the Summit Medical Center in Show Low, Kara nibbled at her thumbnail. With ponderosa pines now silhouetted in twilight, the space seemed colder, even more impersonal than it had been in the late afternoon hours when they'd first arrived.

"This is all my fault." Kara shivered, the memory of the tiff with her mother replaying in her mind. What she'd said. How she'd said it. How stupid she'd been to think there would be time to sit down tonight and talk things out like they always did. "I shouldn't have—"

"You heard the doctor, she's going to be all right." Trey placed a comforting arm around her shoulders, his eyes dark with concern. He was such a sweetheart to stay tonight when Meg had to leave. "It wasn't a full-fledged heart attack, Kara."

But he didn't know about the medical bills. About their argument. How she'd been so upset about her father that she'd treated her mother as she'd had no right to treat her. How the upset could have contributed to her mother's hospitalization.

She fumbled with her handbag, rummaging for her cell phone. "I got hold of Aunt Tammy. She said she'd call the rest of the family. Maybe I should call—"

Who? Dad? No, not Dad.

Tears pricked again. "Now I know how scared Meg must have been when she found Mom that first time. When she couldn't get hold of me right away."

Trey's hand tightened on her shoulder.

"You know where I was then, Trey? In Costa Rica. On a shopping trip for a client. I'd been assigned a company phone, so didn't think to add an international plan to my own."

"You couldn't have known something was going to happen to your mom."

She stuffed her phone back in her handbag. "When Meg finally tracked me down, Mom was awake and calling the shots. Wouldn't let Meg tell me how bad it was. When I spoke to Mom she insisted it was no biggie. Not that serious. That I shouldn't rush back. So I didn't."

"Moms can be like that sometimes."

"I almost died when I walked in and saw her at the Thanksgiving dinner at the RV park. In a wheelchair. Oxygen. Frail looking. I'd have come, Trey, I would have."

"There's no doubt in my mind that you would have."

"But why didn't I learn my lesson? I could tell she seemed tired the last week or two. I'd ask her if everything was okay and she'd always say, 'sure, I'm fine, doll.' But she wasn't and I should have known it. I was too busy chomping at the bit to get back to Chicago. Only saw and heard what I wanted to."

He frowned. "You're not a doctor."

"No, but I *am* a daughter. And a daughter should—" Her voice cracked, and her gaze sought his for reassurance. "We had a fight last night. About my dad. Apparently he's been helping her out—monetarily— off and on through the years. Which didn't go over real big with me."

Trey pulled his arm from around her, clasped his hands and leaned forward to rest his forearms on his knees. "You know, Kara, maybe it's not my place to say anything, but when I first met you, it didn't take a whole lot of smarts to recognize your dad's abandonment did a number on you."

"That obvious?"

"Still is." He cleared his throat. "Maybe it's time to set yourself free of him."

"Oh, believe me, I've tried."

"I don't mean shoving him under the rug. Forgetting about him. I don't think you'll ever have much success with that." He took her hand in his, his gaze earnest. "Have you ever thought about letting it go? Forgiving him?"

She jerked her hand away, staring at him in disbelieving silence. Was he out of his mind?

"You and your mom came close to parting ways after a fight about him. Isn't that reason enough?"

With a harsh laugh, she shook her head.

"Forgive him? For what he did to me and Mom?" She stood, trying to get as far away from him as she could. "Do you have any idea what it was like for me? Waking up in the middle of the night and hearing my mom crying? For *years?* To be subject to the curious looks. Hear the whispered—and not so whispered—speculation about his departure. Why he dumped Mom. Didn't he even care enough for me to arrange shared custody?"

"I'm not saying it will be easy." He stood up as well. "I'm not saying he deserves it. But forgiveness isn't something you do for him, it's something you do for yourself. For your mom."

"You don't know him, Trey, or you wouldn't suggest such a thing."

"Kara Dixon?" A pastel-clad nurse had stepped

into the room and they both turned toward her, Kara's heart slamming in her chest.

"I'm Kara."

"Your mother would like to see you. But for just a few minutes, please."

Kara exchanged a quick look with Trey, then on unsteady legs followed the nurse down a long, glossy-floored hallway to the intensive care unit. Behind a curtained-off area, with a blanket pulled up to her neck and a tangle of tubes and wires surrounding her, Mom looked weak and defenseless.

"Hey, doll." Her voice barely registered above a whisper, but her eyes warmed.

With a shaky breath, Kara approached and took the familiar hand in a gentle clasp. Hardly any grip at all in the once-firm fingers. "Hey, Mom. You sure gave me a scare. This is getting to be a habit you're going to have to break."

"Humph." Mom produced a faint smile. "Trey. He out there? Waiting room?"

She nodded. Why mention Trey at a time like this?

"Good man," her mother said, studying her with barely open eyes. "Just sayin'."

"Sayin' too much if you ask me." She tucked the blanket in around her. "We're only allowed a few minutes."

"Telling you, Kara…" She was rapidly losing alertness. Probably the meds.

"I've contacted Aunt Tammy and Brielle. They're coming."

"Heard about…tune up?"

She nodded. "More stents. Tomorrow morning."

"Not good. Warehouse. Bad for business, this being sick."

She patted her mother's hand. "I have it covered, Mom."

"No. You need…Chicago."

"I need to be here."

Mom's grip tightened. Barely. "Don't want…giving up dream."

"Like you gave up yours?" Kara kicked herself for the insensitive reminder even as she spoke the words.

"Wanted other dream. More." A smile touched Mom's lips. "Wife to your dad. Mother to you."

"And look where that got you." She forced a teasing lilt into her words. "Podunk Springs."

"Fond…Podunk Springs." Mom coughed. Another trembling smile. "Got me a daughter…proud of, too."

Pain slashed through her and she drew a ragged breath. "Oh, Mom, I'm so sorry we argued. I—"

Her mother nodded. Closed her eyes. The frail hand relaxed.

Tears pricked as Kara leaned down to kiss her now-sleeping mother's forehead. Proud? Mom wouldn't be proud of her if she knew how deeply she despised

Dad. And what she'd done to Trey. Was still doing to him.

And how much she resented being stuck in Canyon Springs.

Chapter Fourteen

"Where are you?" a terse but familiar voice demanded through her cell phone receiver.

Spence. Monday. She glanced at her watch and groaned. Two o'clock. Chicago time. Oh, no.

"Didn't you get my message?" She glanced over at Trey, then at Meg, Aunt Tammy and cousin Brielle who'd driven in from Prescott last night. At Bill Diaz, who'd just walked in. "Mom's been hospitalized. A near heart attack."

"So, when are you rescheduled to get in?"

Did he not hear what she just said?

"Mom came close to another heart attack, Spence. I can't leave until I make sure she's okay."

"So what—a day or two?"

"I don't know. She had a couple of stents placed a short while ago. Hasn't come out from the anesthetic yet."

A lengthy silence echoed on the other end. She took a steadying breath, blinking back the tears forming in her eyes. This was it, wasn't it? He was gathering his thoughts, his words, to tell her to forget the promotion. His mentorship. Maybe even a job.

She uttered a silent prayer. God had been hearing from her a lot in the past forty-eight hours. "Spence?"

His sigh carried clearly over the miles. "Look, I'm sorry. I'm not taking all this in yet. Expected you on that flight."

"I know. I'm sorry. I—"

"No problem. It's understandable. I needed to get out of the studio anyway."

"Gabrielle is still pressuring you?"

"What do you think? But don't worry about it. You have other things to deal with now. I'll take care of Gabrielle."

"Thanks. I'm really sorry."

"Yeah, well, take care of yourself. And your Mom. Get back here as fast as you can."

"I will. I promise. And thanks again." She shut off the phone.

"Your boss giving you a hard time?" Trey's tone held a protective ring. He was all but glowering.

"I can't believe you had to tell him twice about your mom's condition," Bill Diaz, Meg's soon-to-be father-in-law, shook his head. He'd been friends with Kara's mom for years, although Kara had long hoped they'd be more than friends.

"Don't worry. It's all good." At least that's what she kept telling herself. "It's just that he's my supervisor.

Mentor. And he's trying to hold a promotion open for me."

"I'd like to give him a piece of my mind," Aunt Tammy mumbled as she looked up from the magazine clutched in her hands. "Don't have any patience with big-city bullies."

Kara laughed. "Honestly, he's a sweet guy. He's just trying to protect my interests."

Trey snorted.

"Is he cute?" Brielle popped the top of her third diet soda and shook back her shoulder-length brown hair.

"Mmm. I think you'd think so."

"He's not blond, is he? I think blond guys look sickly."

Kara laughed again. It felt good. Her thoughts had been so wrapped up with Mom, her nerves stretched to their limits. "He has light brown hair, but he's not blond."

"Good. If you decide you don't want him, send him my way." Brielle winked, then glanced at Trey. "Or any extras you may happen to have on hand."

Meg gathered up her book bag—she'd taken a personal day from work but had been constructing lesson plans at the hospital. "Anyone care to join me in the cafeteria? I could use some lunch."

Kara begged off, but Aunt Tammy, Brielle and Bill departed with her. Trey moved from the most distant chair in their cluster and eased down beside her.

"I'd be happy to pick up something for you to eat

if cafeteria food doesn't appeal. Pick any restaurant within a hundred miles. It's yours for the asking."

"Thanks, but I'm not hungry. Feel a little queasy."

"I'll take on that Spence guy if that would help. Don't care much for a man who makes a woman cry."

He'd seen how close she'd come to that?

"I'm okay. A little emotional, I guess."

"Not surprising." He glanced around the room at several other clusters of family and friends waiting anxiously for reports on loved ones. "So, do you still think you'll head back to the Midwest after your mom's latest setback?"

"Like I told Spence, I have to see how Mom comes through this. The way she looked this morning before they rolled her in for the procedure, she's not going to be up to managing the Warehouse anytime soon."

"Maybe you can hire a manager to fill in for you."

"Maybe." But that wasn't likely. A manager would need a living wage, and with Mom's precarious financial situation…well, her daughter could work for free. "I'll stick around awhile longer. See how it goes."

"You doing okay, though? Financially I mean? Being away from your job this long has to be rough."

She dropped her gaze to her hands, fearful he might glimpse the alarm in her eyes. "I'm dipping into my savings. Still have expenses in Chicago even in my absence."

"What I can pay won't foot the bill for a cham-pagne-and-caviar diet, but I could use your continued office help. As much time as you can spare. You type fifty times faster than I do."

She needed the extra money. But could she manage to look out for the Warehouse and Mom, keep up with the Garson Design project *and* pick up additional hours helping Trey, too? Maybe if she gave up sleep altogether.

She smiled at him, forcing herself to meet his concerned look with a reassuring one of her own. "That's sweet of you, but I'll be fine."

It was one thing to have helped him out for a few days when Marilu left as thanks for his assistance at the Warehouse. But she couldn't let herself become further indebted to a man whose reputation she'd all but reduced to rubble.

Nor could she let her heart become more attached to his.

"Not so fast, son."

"It's all right here." Trey tapped the thick folder of papers he'd placed on the city councilman's desk. "Documented. Notarized. Everything you asked for."

And it was only Thursday. Beat the old guy's arbitrary deadline by a full day, even without Kara's help this week.

Reuben Falkner, dressed more for a round of golf than a winter day in mountain country, pushed back in his cushioned office chair. A stocky, crew-cutted guy in his late sixties, he still carried a no-nonsense demeanor left over from his Marine Corps days. Trey had heard he was a former MP—military police-man—a role he continued as a guardian of Canyon Springs.

"This isn't a done deal, you understand. Need to review everything. Weigh the impact on the community."

"You're the only member of the city council who has objections. The documentation here is complete. Thorough."

"Not objections, Mr. Kenton. Concerns."

"Duffy Logan's place was a valued part of the community for years." Trey kept his tone low, respectful.

"And so it was. But times have changed since Duffy first developed that property over a quarter of a century ago. The area's built up around it. There's greater awareness of the environment now. More comprehensive regulations."

"You'll find I've observed those to the letter. I plan to follow in the footsteps of Duffy's reputation. Build on it."

The man chuckled. "Funny you should mention reputation given that you have quite the reputation yourself."

Realization sliced through Trey. So this was Reuben

Falkner's agenda? To let him get this far along in the process only to refuse final approval because of something that happened over a decade ago? Something he didn't have anything to do with?

"I'm known for my honesty, sir. Integrity."

The older man leaned forward. "That's not what goes through the minds of most people in this community when they hear the name Trey Kenton."

He stiffened and met the almost-amused gaze of the councilman. "Would you care to clarify that?"

Reuben adjusted his glasses to peer over the top of them. "It's ironic, wouldn't you say, that you'll be earning your living off the property you attempted to destroy when it belonged to another man?"

"You're opposing this project based on an unfounded accusation?"

"Unfounded? You may not have ended up with a jail term, what with your father being a preacher and Duffy letting you off the hook. But you know starting a fire isn't an easily forgiven offense in these parts. You could have burned the town to the ground. *Unfounded accusation* is hardly the term I'd use for it. You were all but caught red-handed."

"But I wasn't. And that's because I'm innocent."

The councilman made a shooing motion. "I'm not opposing you on this, so don't go whining about it around town. It takes time for a thorough review. That's all I'm saying. I'm a busy man."

"These permits are the final piece to wrap things

up. Start the hiring process. Bring jobs and tourist dollars to Canyon Springs by summer."

"I'm fully aware of that, Mr. Kenton. It's a noble cause you're spearheading. Your plan to employ locals is commendable." The phone on his desk rang and he reached for it. "But Rome wasn't built in a day. I'll be in touch."

A sharp retort formed in Trey's mind, but with a brisk nod, he departed. Seething.

Now what, God? He'd done just about everything that could be done on the project until he got the final go-aheads. The men who'd hired him expected the facility to be up and running by the time summer visitors returned to the high country. May. June at the latest. He'd tentatively booked several events for the indoor arena. Riding lessons. Horse sale. Barrel racing clinic. Calf roping classes. Had a waiting list for people planning to board their horses.

Out on the main street, he strode toward his own office. You'd think in a town this size the red tape would be diminished. But due to some obscure law on the books, a single councilman could put the brakes on a legitimate business endeavor even when every other governmental entity under the sun had given it the go-ahead.

"Penny for your thoughts, Cowboy," a melodious female voice called, teasing his ears as he crossed over to the Warehouse side of the street.

He swung around to find a smiling, bundled-up

Kara standing outside the door, arms laden with two banker-size boxes.

She raised her delicate brows. "And from the look on your face, those thoughts must be a humdinger."

"You're back." His heart lightened as he hurried forward to take the boxes into his own arms. But up close he recognized signs of fatigue in her pretty face. "How's your mom?"

"Improving by the minute. But even though this episode wasn't as bad as the first one, they want to keep her at the hospital until Monday for observation." She made a face. "Insurance company will love that."

"Then back to physical therapy?"

Kara nodded. "So I'll be sticking around awhile longer."

"Did your boss hassle you about that?" If she said yes, he'd catch the next flight to Chicago and practice roping and tying on the jerk.

She grimaced. "Haven't told him yet. Thought I'd wait until Mom's released and I can get a feel for how things are going."

"So, where're you headed with these boxes?"

"Need to take some paperwork home and get it organized." She pointed to her mom's SUV parked a few doors down and he headed off, with her beside him. She cast him a weary smile. "So what's going on in your world that made you look like a thundercloud?"

"Had a run-in with one of our good councilmen."

Her smile melted. "Reuben? What's he objecting to now?"

"He's not objecting to anything. He has *concerns*." Trey could hear the sarcasm oozing from his own words.

"Such as?"

"Same things he belabored earlier. Repercussions on similar businesses. Signage regulations. Property lighting standards—you know, since this is a Dark Sky City. Wants to take another look at the environmental impact. Drainage. Noise. *Odors*."

"Like he's a competent judge of any of those things?" She threw up her hands in apparent exasperation. "You got the go-ahead on the environmental impact analysis before you even started. Even the city planner said no problem with retaining the property's original use. And what similar businesses is he talking about?"

They stopped at the back of the SUV where Kara popped the back gate open. He placed the boxes inside, then straightened.

"Seems his prime 'concern' is the reputation of the new manager."

"He said that?" She closed the vehicle gate and steadied herself against it with her hand.

"Thinks I got off scot-free because of my dad's connections. Sees himself as the great benevolent protector of Canyon Springs."

"He's always been that way. Sometimes it's appreciated, but this is harassment. Even if he doesn't believe you're innocent, can't he see you're a grown man now? Deserve a second chance? And look at the jobs this project has already generated."

"He says my intention along those lines is—and I quote—commendable. But I guess that's not enough to overshadow what he's convinced is a blot on my past."

Kara thrust her hands into her jacket pockets. "The mayor is an old friend of Mom's. Maybe I could talk to him. See if he'd light a fire under Reuben."

"Thanks, but I don't want to rile the old guy any more than I have to. He looks like the kind who'd dig in for a siege if he felt challenged." He leaned back on the SUV and crossed his arms. "I'm trying to see things from his perspective. To look at this from a professional standpoint rather than taking it personal."

"Sounds like Reuben's making it personal."

Sounded like it to him, too. But he shouldn't have said anything to Kara about it—whining like the aging former MP warned him against. He took a steadying breath and changed the subject. "You know, Kara, I've been following your advice, backing off from asking questions of locals regarding the fire."

She nodded, but her expression looked wary, as if waiting for the other shoe to drop.

"But I can't stand here twiddling my thumbs and let those old lies abort this project. I have too much riding on it. So do the investors who hired me."

He rubbed his forehead, waiting her for her to jump

in with dire warnings. But she only stared at him like a proverbial deer caught in the headlights. "So while I know you and Jason have my best interests at heart, I don't have any choice but to stir things up. See what I can do to smoke out the person who really started the fire before it's too late."

If it wasn't already too late.

Chapter Fifteen

Before she could take in what he'd said, her cell phone went off, playing a merry tune. She grabbed it out of her coat pocket to view the caller ID. Spence.

Just what she didn't need.

"I'm sorry, Trey, I have to take this call."

His eyes filled with concern. "The hospital?"

"No, Chicago." She put the phone to her ear and headed for the Warehouse door. "Hey, Spence. How goes it?"

"That's my question for you," her boss countered. "How's your mother?"

She entered the building, relieved rather than worried that there were no customers this morning. "She's doing well, considering. Will remain in the hospital until next week."

"Then she can come home? And you can get back here?"

Kara wandered among the aisles, straightening displays with her free hand as she moved toward the back of the store. "She can't be left by herself right away. And there's no one to manage her business."

"I know what you're going through. How hard it is to live and work so far from family." He paused. "But sometimes you have to step back and let others take responsibility. Carry some of the load. My dad died last year and I couldn't get away from here to help out in L.A. All his care fell on my sisters."

"I don't have any sisters. Or brothers."

"I'm just saying, Kara—"

"Spence, I'm entitled by law—"

"To unpaid leave time. I know that. I'm just giving you a heads-up. This isn't a good time to be away from the home base."

"What do you mean?"

He lowered his voice, as if wary of eavesdroppers. "I'm hearing layoffs are coming. Deep ones. In this economy, our high-end clientele is cutting back. Even if their finances weathered the storm, big CEOs don't want their names in the paper or faces on TV pointing out that they had a million-dollar office or home makeover the same month they laid off workers or cut benefits."

"They'd be pumping money into the economy. That's good, right?"

"But nobody wants to risk it—you know, fearful of that 'let them eat cake' label. It's bad for business."

"So I'm getting laid off." She should have seen it coming. She'd missed so much work this past year she'd be a prime target, would disappear in an avalanche of layoffs.

"Nothing's certain. But we're all being scrutinized. There's not enough work to go around."

"And I'm one of the newer kids on the block."

"And one who doesn't have a physical presence here right now, who isn't out on the streets drumming up business."

"I'm laying the groundwork on the NuTowne office project for you. Working on it every free minute I can get."

"Don't waste any more time on it. Just heard they're floundering. Big-time. So the new facility won't get off the ground." Spence sighed. "Sorry to be the bearer of bad news, but you need to get back here, kiddo. Pronto."

Kiddo. No "little cowgirl."

"Believe me, I want to. But I'm needed here. I'll have to rethink things. Figure out my options. See what kind of arrangements I can make for my mother."

"Just don't wait too long. I'm slipping in reminders of your contributions to the team. How you hustled on the design research and presentation to help me bring that Barrington contract in. And Tellmont."

"Thanks. I'm sorry I'm letting you down."

He lowered his voice even further. "You're not letting me down if you get yourself back here ASAP. Like yesterday."

"Spence—"

"Just get back here. Now. Gotta run. *Ciao.*"

The line went dead in her ear.

She shut off the phone and stuffed it back in her pocket. Stared vacantly into space, tears pricking her eyes. What was she going to do? How could she leave now? Mom needed her here. But Mom needed her there, too, didn't she? To funnel money back to pay the medical bills, keep the Warehouse.

"Bad news?"

She whirled to face Trey, standing no more than twelve feet from her. She hadn't even heard the bells above the door when he'd come in. Had he coattailed in right behind her? Heard her side of the whole conversation?

She blinked rapidly and gave a little laugh. "Oh, nothing much. Just that if I don't get back to my job immediately, there may not be a job to go back to, let alone a promotion. Company-wide layoffs are in the works."

He gave a low whistle. "Can they do that? Fire you while you're on leave?"

"I don't know all the legalities. But I'd think if they're having to let others go—" She bit down on her lower lip. *Please, God, don't let me cry in front of Trey.* "Spence says this isn't a good time to be an absentee employee."

"I'm sorry, Kara. I know the job, the promotion, mean everything in the world to you. Your dream ticket out of Canyon Springs."

She swallowed. "Unfortunately, keeping the job

isn't all about a dream anymore. Somehow I have to make arrangements for Mom's care. For management of the Warehouse. It's come to the point where I can do more for her for the long term in Chicago than I can here."

He frowned. "How do you figure that?"

"Because—" She gazed around the expanse of the Warehouse, her lower lip trembling. "No way am I going to let my mom lose this place."

"That's a possibility?"

She nodded, a single tear trickling down her cheek. A real possibility.

That tear—the same wistful, lost expression she'd had when reminiscing about the Warehouse Saturday morning before she left for Show Low—ripped Trey open deeper than the horn of a raging Brahma could ever have done. Without hesitation, he stepped forward and opened his arms. She came willingly, her own arms slipping tightly around him, her face pressing against the collar of his jacket.

"What's going on, Kara?" he said softly, laying the side of his face against the top of her ponytailed head.

"Medical bills are eating her alive." Her voice quavered. "She could lose the Warehouse and she didn't even tell me."

"Are you sure?"

She nodded, her hair brushing his cheek. "I stumbled across the papers Friday night. Overdue notices.

Threats for legal action. And when I confronted her—" so their argument wasn't only about her dad "—she admitted it." Her words ended with a ragged breath.

He tightened his hold on her trembling body, willing his own strength to be infused into her.

"When was she going to tell me, Trey? When I came to visit and found the Warehouse closed? Under new ownership?"

"She must have had her reasons."

"Oh, yeah. She said she didn't want me to worry." She gave a weak, scoffing laugh. "Said she wants me to stay in Chicago to live my dream. But if she'd have said something, I could have been helping all along. Maybe it wouldn't have come to this."

"It probably happened so quickly she didn't have time to think that far." His own mother climbed mountains to keep from worrying him or his brothers about anything. "She probably thought she had things under control. So go easy on her."

The arms around his waist loosened as she pulled back, her fingers tightening on his jacket front. "I didn't go easy on her. At all. I carried on awful, Trey. I was so mad."

"And scared."

She nodded again. "We argued again Saturday night. About Dad. So I stayed as far away from her as I could get on Sunday, trying to get my temper under control. Thought that by Sunday night we'd have both cooled down, could get everything straightened out between us before I left. But then—"

She pulled back and stared at him, eyes filled with fear. "I came a hairbreadth from not having that opportunity, Trey. Will I never learn? She could have died."

"But she didn't. I'd say that's evidence of God's hands-on involvement in your life, Kara, whether you're willing to admit it or not."

She leaned her forehead on his chest. "Maybe."

"It's going to be okay."

"You mean that everything works for the good for those who love God stuff? Sorry, but nice verses and a pep talk won't score any points. This is reality. Mom will lose her livelihood, will probably have to leave Canyon Springs if I can't get these bills paid off."

"That's what you were doing in Show Low Saturday, wasn't it? All dressed up." And looking prettier than any woman had a right to. He felt her nod against him. "So you got a loan?"

She lifted her head. "No. They're stingier than a two-year-old with a favorite toy right now."

"It will be okay," he repeated, mind racing as a plan formulated. He had money set aside. Had practically lived the life of a pauper to save every cent he could to someday buy property. A place to settle down. If he loaned it to Kara, how long would it be before he'd be able accumulate that level of funds again? He didn't doubt that it would be repaid—but it could be years until that time.

But what choice did he have? He couldn't stand to see her like this. "I don't know how much your mom's bills are, but I have a fairly sizable amount of money set aside. It's yours for as long as you need it."

She stared at him, her beautiful eyes searching his. Eyes filled with disbelief. Hope.

And something much more personal.

It slammed into him with the force of a stampeding herd of buffalo.

She slowly leaned forward. Tightened her grip on the front of his jacket. Her mouth inches from his. "Oh, Trey—"

His heart staggered as he lowered his head, his lips barely grazing hers.

This man was so good, so very good. The most decent man she'd ever known and she'd ruined any chance of a relationship with him when she was a stupid teenager.

Nevertheless, heart beating an erratic rhythm, Kara clung to him. Returned his warm, tender kiss with a tentative one of her own. How much sweeter, how much more meaningful than the greedy, demanding ones she'd impulsively pulled him into that night so long ago.

Could there still be a second chance for them? After all the painful detours and guilt-laden years, had God brought them both back to Canyon Springs for a purpose? For her to find forgiveness in Trey's arms? A safe place to come home to? It was as if the stone wall of fear she'd built around her heart crumbled at her feet. Turned to dust.

Thankfulness surged through her. Was this really happening?

After a not-nearly-long-enough moment in his arms, Trey gently pulled back. Stepped back. Released her. His expression troubled.

Just like before.

He swallowed. "I'm sorry, Kara. I don't know what got into me."

That's what he'd said that night, too, even though it had been she who'd thrown herself at him. She stepped back, too, heat flooding her face. What had she been thinking, playing kissy-face right on the sales floor of the Warehouse? What if a customer had walked in on them?

"It's okay," she said softly, as numbness gripped her heart.

He nodded, but didn't look at her. "I, uh, I'm serious about the loan, Kara."

"Thank you. But I think it would be better if—"

"It would be strictly a business transaction, but no interest. Or minimal enough not to raise any IRS flags. It wouldn't have any, you know, personal expectations. No strings attached."

But what if she *wanted* personal expectations? Strings attached?

Stop that. You're such a fool. Letting a kiss intended only to soothe and comfort send her off and running down the yellow brick road to fantasies of forgiveness and happily ever afters. The minute she confessed her role in the teenage deception that dogged him to this day, he'd be out the door. She couldn't accept a loan of that magnitude without telling him the truth.

"I appreciate it, Trey. And you're a sweetheart to offer." She kept her voice level, impersonal. "But I'll get a bank loan when I get back to Chicago."

Assuming she still had a job.

"Think about it, okay? You could go back at least knowing a chunk of the bills are paid. Get the collection people off your mom's back. The stress off both of you."

It was so tempting. An answer to prayer.

But so wrong.

She could never accept his money. And would never be given the opportunity to accept his love.

What was he thinking when he kissed her yesterday?

That was just it, he hadn't been. He seized the moment—and did something really stupid. Just like with Tanya. Flashing red lights all over the place, but he'd ignored them. Again.

Trey surveyed the room at his brother's place that he'd called home for almost six months, then picked up one of the oversize boxes stacked in the corner. With moving day fast approaching for Reyna, Jason and the girls, he needed to get his own stuff hauled into town. Today seemed as good a time as any to begin loading the truck. In hindsight, however, renting the apartment above the Warehouse was another of his less-than-smart moves. Even when Kara left—no employer in their right mind would lay her off—he'd still have a connection to her through her mom. Probably have to hear updates on her career. Promotion. Spence.

But no way would the good Lord have given him the seal of approval on that kiss. It implied things. Things he had no business implying. He and Kara were on totally different wavelengths. City girl. Country boy. And even more significant, he believed God was involved in the smallest details of his life, and Kara denied He did anything beyond setting her world in motion. Attempting to combine those two extremes was a disaster in the making. He didn't need to take one of Jas' premarital surveys to recognize that.

But when he backed off after initiating that kiss, she probably thought he'd been toying with her affections. Disregarding her feelings. One more reason for her not to trust God. Or him.

"What seems to be your problem?" Reyna appeared in the doorway, arms folded and a don't-lie-to-me expression on her face.

"What do you mean?"

"Since you got home last night you've looked like a sad old hound dog who had his bone taken away from him."

Trey shifted the box in his arms. "No bones lost here."

"Could have fooled me." She eyed him skeptically. "Even Mary says you're no fun."

"Just a lot on my mind. Busy man."

"Yeah, right." She started to turn away, then apparently thought better of it. "How's Sharon Dixon?"

Why was she asking him?

"Haven't spoken with her. Heard she'll probably be coming home on Monday."

"Kara still planning to go back to Chicago?"

"Assume so."

Reyna studied him a moment longer, looking as if she wanted to say more. Then she shifted gears. "I have to run to town. You going to be around for a while?"

"Just loading the truck. Thought I'd take some of my stuff in this evening when I go in to feed the horses."

"Would you mind if I left Missy and Mary with you? I have lots of in-and-out errands to run, and you know how convoluted the logistics get when you have to deal with car seats."

"Yeah, sure. But I don't know that Mary will find my hauling boxes out of the house much 'fun.'"

Reyna leaned back against the doorframe. "You're having second thoughts about making a permanent move to Canyon Springs, aren't you?"

Could she read Jason like a book, too? Must drive him nuts.

"Let's put it this way. I'm not making any headway on clearing my name. As much as I need to do it in order to stay here, there isn't much time for digging up, let alone pursuing, leads while I'm trying to keep the renovation on track."

Even though he'd told Kara he planned to renew his investigation, he wasn't a cop. He didn't have the right to point fingers, pull in suspects for interrogation. Couldn't apply pressure for a full confession like a TV private eye. And she was right, it could backfire on him.

"So if you can't find out who set the fire, you'll hire a replacement manager and that's that? You won't stay?"

"I know you want me to settle down here, Reyna. But—"

"Why are you punishing yourself? Making this silly rule or whatever it is that you have to prove your innocence or it's *adiós?*"

"It's not a rule, it's—"

"What is it about Canyon Springs—" she folded her arms, eyes narrowing "—that you're so afraid of?"

He met Reyna's querying gaze. But he couldn't explain it to her. How he'd long dreamed of settling down in one place. How he wanted to be near family. To end the years of a transient lifestyle and short-lived, shallow relationships. Yet at the same time, how much he doubted his own ability to be a success at it.

She looked him over. "It's Kara, isn't it?"

Her words kicked him in the gut. Where'd she come up with this stuff? "What do you mean?"

"You know what I'm talking about. You were getting pretty satisfied with the idea of returning here until she showed up. I didn't catch on immediately, but now looking back I can see—"

"Whatever you see, Reyna, is in your too-vivid imagination."

"Trey! Why can't you ever admit you care for a woman?" Reyna's eyes flashed a challenge. "There's no shame in it."

He set the box on the bed and drew in a steadying breath. "There is when you know God's not in it."

"And just how do you know this?"

"Believe me, I know it."

"So you're punishing yourself for feeling this way—about a woman who doesn't know a great guy when she sees one—by not making a life in Canyon Springs? That doesn't make sense. Why not do something nice for yourself for a change?"

With a look of exasperation, she turned away and headed back down the hallway.

Reyna made it sound so simple.

But it wasn't.

He wanted to settle down here. But how could he ever find a woman who meant more to him than Kara? He couldn't just pick a substitute. That wouldn't be fair to some poor little gal who'd be a pale shadow of the woman who'd claimed his heart since he was seventeen. Would he find himself still dreaming of Kara as he slumbered next to his replacement bride? Would he look at their kids and wonder what his and Kara's would have looked like? Would he find himself secretly longing to glimpse the ponytailed woman each time he heard she was in town?

That kind of "cheating" went against everything he believed in.

Fire. He'd always be playing with fire when it came to Kara. His inner eye flashed to yesterday at the Warehouse. Holding the woman of his dreams so close. His lips on hers…his imagination taking flight in those brief, sweet moments.

Kara as a wife. A mother.

But even if everything else was different, if they shared the same beliefs and values, even if she trusted him to make a commitment to a relationship, how could he ever make her happy in the one place on earth she wanted nothing to do with?

He picked up the box again. It didn't seem right. Getting your heart broken by the same little gal twice. Didn't say a whole lot for his intelligence. His common sense. How'd he get the idea in the first place that he could come back to this town? *Her town.* Pretend nothing had happened to his heart?

The problem was, now he recognized the truth.

He couldn't live in a Canyon Springs that wasn't called home to Kara.

Chapter Sixteen

"We sure could use a real designer like you on the team, Kara. There's been a paid position opening available for months."

High school English teacher Sandi Bradshaw gave her a pleading look as they stood in the frozen food aisle of the local discount store Saturday night. She'd met Sandi, a friend of Meg's, at the New Year's Eve party just over a month ago.

"There are a number of places going into foreclosure," she continued, "but the ones the organization can afford still need major work. Not only elbow grease, but redesign of the spaces. One is the cutest little bungalow, but the rooms are so chopped up. It had originally been a single-family dwelling, then was carved up into office space. We'd like to turn it back into a family home."

"Wish I could help." And surprisingly, she did. The project sounded worthwhile. One that would bring more satisfaction than sprucing up the home or office digs of Chicago's richer than rich. Was this the same group Trey had mentioned being involved with? "Unfortunately, I'll be leaving town as soon as I finish making arrangements for my mom's care."

"So you're going back to Chicago?"

How many times was she going to hear that question? Surely it had to be all over town by now that returning was her intention. Had always been. Did they think if they asked it enough times they'd get a different answer?

"Chicago's home now." Memory flashed to the cramped apartment she shared with her roommates. Calling it "home" was a stretch.

"Think you'll ever move back?" Sandi's cheeks flushed, as though she'd asked a too-personal question. "I mean, I heard you were seeing someone. Trey Kenton."

"What's this about Trey Kenton?" Cate Landreth, a teacher's aide at the high school and a notorious gossip, pulled a pizza carton from the glass-doored freezer next to them.

Of all the dumb luck.

Sandi flashed a look of apology at her. Working at the high school, she'd no doubt figured out by now that Cate had a nose for news—and fabrication when news wasn't handy.

The auburn-haired Cate tossed the pizza in her cart and focused on Kara. "What's up with you and that good-lookin' guy anyway? The suspense is killing me."

Kara managed a benign smile. "Just friends."

"An ex-cowboy isn't good enough for you now that you're a big-city girl?" Cate gave a sharp laugh and nudged Sandi. "Or the fact that he's a pyromaniac?"

Kara's heart jolted. "That's not funny, Cate. Trey didn't start that fire."

Cate dismissed her with a wave of her red-lacquered nails. "Well, pyro or not, he's easy on the eyes, isn't he, girls? Heard he's thinking of settling down in Canyon Springs after he gets Duffy's old place up and running. That true, Kara?"

"Don't know what he's decided." She wasn't doling out insider information on Trey. She owed him that much.

"Heard he's looking at property, too." The woman kept her gaze pinned on Kara. "Must have done pretty well on the rodeo circuit to build up a nest egg."

When Kara merely shrugged, Cate zeroed in on Sandi, a speculative gleam in her eyes. "You know what Jane Austen said, don't you? 'It is a truth universally acknowledged, that a single man in possession of a good fortune, must be in want of a wife.' So now's your chance, Sandi."

Cate's too-loud laugh echoed as Sandi blushed a becoming shade of pink and darted anxious eyes in Kara's direction.

Kara's throat constricted as an image flashed through her mind of the pretty, satin-clad blonde coming down the church aisle on Trey's arm. Both laughing. Eyes only for each other. Him pausing to lean down for a long, lingering kiss.

"Meg!" Cate waved as she spied Meg McGuire-soon-to-be-Diaz, approaching pushing an empty shopping cart. "We're deciding how to divvy up Trey Kenton among the single female population of Canyon Springs. Care to be included or do you think you'll stick with that Diaz fellow?"

Meg laughed, but the questioning look she turned in Kara's direction was volleyed back at her with a get-me-out-of-here stare. "Trey's a sweetie, but no way am I trading in Joe."

"Kara's turned up her citified nose at him. Sandi's too chicken to make her move." The redhead glanced at herself in the frozen food glass door, fluffing her hair. "I'd go after him myself if wasn't for my Duke. Show that cowboy what a real woman is."

Meg spun her cart in the direction from which she'd come, and for a moment Kara panicked. *Don't leave me here with Cate.*

"Kara? Weren't you going to show me those kitchen accessories? The ones you thought might be nice for the parsonage housewarming?"

Thank you, thank you, thank you.

"Right. I'd totally forgotten."

"Shoppin' for your preacher's place?" Cate stepped back as Kara, shopping basket looped over her arm, slipped past her.

"Just getting ideas." Meg smiled brightly as they

turned to head down the aisle. "See you Monday, Cate. Sandi."

But Sandi had slipped off in the opposite direction.

They made their way to the back of the store, sharing only "a look" until they were well out of range of Cate.

"What was that all about?" Meg whispered.

"Cate was feeling me out about where I stood with Trey."

Meg's hand flew to her mouth. "Oh, dear. What did you tell her? Not much, I hope."

"The truth. That he and I are friends."

Her brows knit together. "Do you think that was wise throwing the door open to the competition? Sandi, I mean."

"I'm not competing for—" she glanced around and lowered her voice "—him. Besides, I can't see Sandi as his match."

"Why not? She's a delightful gal. Cute. Better-than-nice figure, too, and don't kid yourself that men don't notice that. You wouldn't believe all the insider stuff I've learned about the male perspective from Joe this past month." Meg rolled her eyes. "She has a sweet daughter and Trey loves kids. Plus it's a small town and she's available."

Kara smiled, determined that her friend wouldn't detect her muddled feelings for Trey. "Then I wish her luck."

"You may smile now, but let me tell you he's ripe

for the picking. He wants to settle down. Raise a family. Don't forget, it was only a few months ago that he asked me out. So it's not like he's going to wait around forever for a Mrs. Right."

"We don't think of each other in that way, Meg." Or at least she wouldn't confess to it. But Thursday's kiss still lingered on her lips. Kept her awake at night.

"What do you mean? I saw the way he looked at you at the parsonage a few weeks ago. Haven't you even noticed?"

She had, but Meg didn't understand. Would never understand why there could be no future for her and Trey.

"Look, Kara, Sandi would never horn in on somebody else's relationship. But—"

"I'm going back to Chicago. Like I told you in college—and the story hasn't changed—I have no intention of being tied down to Canyon Springs. By anything or anyone."

Not even Trey.

Trey looked up from the bedding display just as Meg and Kara rounded the end of the store aisle.

How did Kara manage to look like a knockout even when shopping at a discount place? He'd only glimpsed her a time or two since that memorable morning at the Warehouse, and now, in spite of himself, his eyes drank in the welcome sight of her.

But don't forget, buddy, you're playing with fire.

"Good evening, ladies."

The two women exchanged uncertain glances. Must not have expected to find a man in the housewares department. Or had Kara told Meg he'd kissed her? Didn't best friends tell all?

An unexpected warmth crept up his neck to his ears.

Meg pointed at the plastic-encased, puffy bedspread gripped in his hands. "Pink becomes you, Trey."

He returned her smile, thankful for the distraction, and returned the package to the shelf. "Trying to find something for my nieces' new room. Told Reyna I'd outfit it. There's two of this one in a single-bed size. But I can't find matching stuff."

Meg made a face. "Don't look at me. That's Kara's department."

An unsmiling Kara exchanged a look with her friend, then moved down the aisle to pull out a set of sheets.

"You could always get plain cream. Or white." She met his too-eager gaze with an impersonal one of her own. But he could tell by the way her well-manicured fingers fluttered as she pointed out the wrinkle-free, no-iron labeling, that the kiss wasn't far from her mind either. Had she forgiven him for his impulsive act? Or did she think he was a real jerk?

"You could embroider that same rose design that's on the bedspread along the hems," she continued. "Or trim them with eyelet and weave a pink satin ribbon through the holes."

"Embro? Eye what?" Trey raised his eyebrows and Meg laughed.

"I think he wants you to speak English, Kara."

Kara finally smiled and, even though it wasn't directed at him, his spirits rose. "Since Reyna's mother can make bridal wear, I imagine she can handle embellishing simple sheets."

"Or *you* could," Meg chimed in with a pointed glance in Kara's direction.

"Would you have time?" Trey looked to her for confirmation, trying not to appear too much like a starving man hoping for a handout. What was wrong with him? He shouldn't be asking her for help. Shouldn't be setting the stage to see her more often than necessary.

She studied the package again. "I don't know. Mom will be coming home Monday. And I have a lot to do to get ready to leave."

"Come on," Meg cajoled, "you're a marvel at this stuff."

Kara cast him an uncertain look as she put the sheet set back on the shelf. "I guess it wouldn't take too long. Especially if I did the eyelet. Except for threading the ribbon, it would be mostly machine sewn."

"You'd make some little girls very happy." And a big boy even happier. He didn't know anything about this girlie stuff.

"There now, we're all set," Meg chimed in once more, sending a knowing glance darting his way. His ears warmed again. *Had* Kara told her? "Look, you two, I have to run. Need to pick up Davy from his grandpa's. But you can check out the sewing department and pick out the supplies tonight."

He caught the dismay that flashed through Kara's eyes. Came to her rescue. "I need to run, too. I, uh, have to—do some stuff."

"You can't beg for help, then expect the woman to do everything." Meg grabbed two of the bedspreads he'd been looking at and dropped them in her still-empty cart. Pushed it at Trey. "Get the sheets and there you go."

Kara met his look with one of amused resignation.

A smile tugged as he gripped the cart handle and gave it a shove. Paused to pick up two white sheet sets. Then offered his arm as a chivalrous gentleman might. "Shall we?"

She didn't take him up on his offer, but gave Meg another "look" and took off for the sewing department. Reluctantly, he followed at her pretty heels.

She must have been keen to get this over with, too, for in no time at all she'd checked the measurements on the sheets and pillowcases, and pulled out an oblong roll of three-inch wide white fabric. Kind of puckered, with rounded, holed ridges on two sides and a series of square holes down the middle. She held it up.

"Eyelet." Then she reached for a roll of pink shiny ribbon. "And this is what I'll weave through the square holes. Then sew it down along the hems of the pillows and sheets. Voilà!"

"Voilà!" he echoed, like he knew what she was talking about. "Thanks for doing this. I know you don't have a lot of free time."

"Actually, I have more time than before. Spence said to stop killing myself on the project I've been working on. Guess the client is backing out due to financial issues."

"Rough times for a lot of people."

"That's an understatement."

He absently rearranged the bedspreads in the cart as he considered how best to reapproach an issue he'd given additional thought to. "You know, Kara, I was serious about a loan. Even if it's just enough to cover the Warehouse mortgage for a while until you get back on your feet in Chicago. One less thing to worry about."

She met his questioning gaze with an unsure one of her own. "I think that would complicate things, don't you?"

"You mean because of what happened this past week." He cleared his throat. "Between us."

Color rose in her cheeks and she nodded.

Why was he pushing this? Riding to the rescue just like he'd done with Tanya when she'd fallen behind on her car payments. Now here he was trying to get himself tied down to Kara when he knew better. Needed to let her go.

He grasped the cart handle. "But we're both grown-ups, right?"

"Right," she agreed, although her tone remained doubtful.

"Well, then?"

"I may not have a job when I get back there. Chicago is overflowing with big design firms, and I'd try to get on with another one of them. But in this economy I'd likely be hired at entry level again. Which means entry-level salary, too."

"Yeah, but—"

"Thank you, Trey." Her beautiful eyes, filled with regret, held his. "I can't tell you how much I appreciate your thoughtfulness. But no. And please don't ask again."

Chapter Seventeen

"Shh." A smiling Reyna placed a finger to her lips as she ushered Kara into the newly remodeled parsonage the following Wednesday afternoon. "It's nap time."

"I'm here to drop off something for Trey," Kara whispered, inhaling the "new house" scent as she maneuvered a festively wrapped copy paper box through the door.

"The bedding?" Reyna silently clapped her hands. "He told me what you were doing. It's a surprise, so I'll hide it in my bedroom."

Reyna took the box from her arms. "Be back in a minute."

When she returned, she again placed a finger to her lips and motioned for Kara to follow. What was up? They all but tippy-toed through the house, then at a wide arched doorway Reyna stepped back and motioned her forward.

There in the middle of the family room, under

a quilt-draped card table, lay a sleeping Missy and Mary—and Trey. All three snuggled up together, their heads pillowed on a folded blanket.

Whoever would have thought to find the rough-and-tumble cowboy so vulnerable? The lion beside the lambs. "How precious."

"I just got back from running errands and found them like this," Reyna whispered. "I think they were pretending to camp while they watched *The Little Mermaid*. Fell asleep."

They stood gazing down at the scene for a few moments longer, then Kara followed Reyna back to the living room.

"You should take a picture of them like that."

"Already did. It will make Trey a great Christmas present."

"He'll love it." Kara reached for the screen door latch and let herself out onto the front porch.

"Trey said you're heading back to Chicago."

"As soon as I can."

"I'd hoped you'd stay even after you get your mom back on her feet. You'd be a good distraction for Trey." Reyna stepped out on the porch and closed the door behind her. "You know, from this so-called investigation of his."

"I'm afraid nothing or no one can distract him from that."

"Well, he's getting discouraged. Maybe it's a bargain between him and God or something, this proving his innocence obsession. Who knows what's going on in that man's head. But he's having second thoughts about staying in Canyon Springs after Duffy's is up and running."

"Surely he won't let that stop him. He's said so often how much he wants to be close to his nieces."

"They love having him here, too. But somehow he thinks if he stays but isn't vindicated, it will negatively affect them."

Like her dad leaving town under a cloud did her? Goodness knows she'd hammered that into Trey's head. No wonder he was second-guessing his decision to stick around. Was there no end to how she could mess up this man's life?

"Do you think you could talk to him, Kara? Convince him he's not thinking straight? I think he'd listen to you."

"He won't, Reyna." And she needed to keep out of this. Just because Canyon Springs wasn't her dream, that didn't mean it couldn't be Trey's. Although she still doubted it would work out for him in the long run.

"Maybe I shouldn't say anything, but—" the pretty brunette glanced back at the door "—I have to admit I was thrilled when Mary started talking to him about kissing in connection to ponytails—and you."

Kara's eyes widened and a warm sensation pulsed through her neck as last week's kiss flashed through her mind.

"Oh, I'm sorry. I didn't mean to embarrass you. But I was kind of hoping—I mean, I know for a fact he hasn't been involved seriously with a woman in years. Not since Tanya."

"Tanya?" Her heart contracted with a jealousy she denied at once.

"Oops. I'd better shut up before I get myself in hot water. He'll kill me for talking behind his back. He's such a great guy and I want him to be happy. Right here in Canyon Springs."

"Then you'd better look for a lady love for him elsewhere, Reyna, because as soon as my cousin Brielle gets here to watch over the Warehouse and I can take Mom down to her sister's place in Prescott, I'm out of here."

It sounded so hard-hearted. Selfish. She knew that's what Reyna—and others—would think. That she was abandoning her responsibilities. Her Mom. Just like her dad had done. But what choice did she have? No place in Canyon Springs would pay her nearly as much as Garson Design did. She needed to get those bills paid off. Save the Warehouse.

And keep her heart out of harm's way.

"Hey, there, gal!" Jason Kenton stepped through the store's door during the noon hour the next day, carrying a large clasped envelope. "Where's my brother gotten himself off to?"

Kara looked up from where she'd been stocking shelves near the front counter. "I haven't seen him in days. He's not upstairs?"

"His place is locked up tight." Jason set the envelope

on the counter. "Found this on the top shelf of his closet when I did a walk-through of the cabin this morning. Looks like business papers. Didn't want to leave it on the landing where just anyone could find it—do you mind hanging on to it until he shows up?"

"Be happy to. So, are you glad to be back in town again? Not having to haul water anymore?" That was a disadvantage to living outside the city limits in many high country Arizona locations. Having to transport hundreds of gallons of water in huge poly tanks secured in the beds of pickups or trailers.

"Definitely won't miss that, but sure did appreciate the Phoenix resident who offered his summer cabin to us. So what's your timetable for getting your mom situated at her sister's?"

Reyna must have filled him in, and she braced herself for a sermon on honoring your parents. "I'll take her to Prescott on Monday, then catch a flight to Chicago the next day."

"I'll get over to see her before she leaves then," he said, heading toward the door.

"Great. She'll love that."

That was one thing she *did* like about a small town. The concern and personal attention when illness or injury struck. She'd gotten calls from at least half a dozen friends of Mom, wanting to know what they could do to help.

Shortly after five she was closing up when she heard the creak of the floor upstairs and remembered

Trey's envelope. She grabbed it, locked up and headed to his place. Still seemed strange to have him living up there now, even though he'd been working out of the office for almost a month.

The door off the landing stood partially open and she could hear Trey's voice. Sounded like he was on the phone. She peeked in and saw him standing by the window, his back to her. No need to bother him, she'd just leave her delivery on the desk and slip out.

"Good point," he said, as she pushed the door open wider. "I'm thinking we should set up a conference call next week, get the rest of the investors' take on it."

She tiptoed across the room behind him. Sounded as if he had one of the guys who'd financed the equine center on the line. One of his bosses.

"No, no, I'll handle it. Get it all set up."

She placed the envelope on his desk, then turned to go.

"Well, I appreciate that," he continued. "Sure, sure. Talk to you later, Dix."

With a sharp intake of breath, she halted.

Dix?

Everybody called her father "Dix." Dix's Woodland Warehouse was even named after him. But there could be lots of people, cowboy-type people, named "Dix." Right? He could even be talking to a "Dixie" for all she knew.

At that moment Trey turned from the window, pocketing his phone as he started across the floor.

Then he saw her standing by his desk and stopped dead in his tracks. She'd always heard of blood draining from someone's face, but now she'd seen it with her own eyes. And recognized the truth.

"You know my dad."

He took a deep breath. "Oh, man."

"My dad—he's one of the investors, isn't he?"

Trey ran a hand through his hair. Then nodded, an unhappy man if there ever was one. "I'm sorry, Kara. I—"

"How long have you known him?" Her mind raced to all the times she'd dissed her dad in Trey's presence. She'd made it more than clear how she felt about that man. How could he have kept his connection to him a secret from her? Betrayed her like this?

"Quite a while."

"As in days? Months? Years?"

Trey cleared his throat, his forlorn gaze never leaving hers. "I met him on the rodeo circuit when I was starting out. He sort of took me under his wing—"

A little cry escaped her lips. His confession sickened her.

"I wanted to tell you right out of the chute, Kara. When you first came back. But I'd promised Dix I wouldn't tell anyone in town he was partnering in the business."

She shook her head in disbelief.

"He was afraid with what went on here before that if his name was associated with our project there would be resistance from the community. That it might be harder for us to get it off the ground."

"So you couldn't tell *me?*"

"Dix said you might—"

"Rat him out? Throttle *you?*"

He stretched out his hand in appeal. "He's trying to make it up to the town, to the investors of that earlier debacle. Make things right."

"Like that's possible?" She took a step back. "I don't want to hear any more of this."

"Believe me, I understand—"

"Obviously you don't or you wouldn't have deceived me. No wonder you've been at me to kiss and make up with him—he's been badgering me for years to let him back into my life. Now you're on his payroll, paid to do his bidding."

"Kara, that's not—"

"You may like to think of yourself as a man of integrity. A man of honesty. You may not tolerate anyone lying to you—Marilu, Mary—but you're lying to yourself, you know that? How could you betray me like this?"

Tension hung almost tangibly in the silence.

"You should talk," he said at last, his words devoid of emotion. "You know all about deception yourself."

Her heart all but stopped. Had he found out about Lindi and the fire? About her part in it? "What—what do you mean?"

"You know what I'm talking about." He took a few

steps in her direction. "Your dad hurt you and now you think you can hurt him by not forgiving him. But you're deceiving yourself. Hurting yourself even more than you are him."

"You don't know anything about it, Trey. What he put me and my mother through. The shame I had to live with because of him."

"Maybe not. But I can see how your attempts to keep him at a distance reflect in all you do. I mean look at your career choice—your pursuit of the dream in Chicago."

"What's that have to do with anything?"

"You've chosen a career far from Canyon Springs so you don't have to be reminded of your dad. A career where you can control the outcome, paint things any color you want, gloss over anything you don't want to look at. Make it all pretty." He shook his head and took another step toward her. "And you think that by denying that God has anything to do with the details of your life that you can shut Him out, too."

"You have no right—"

"Friends have rights, Kara."

"Friends? Is that what we are? You could have fooled me at the Warehouse a week ago. Or was that part of a standard comfort-and-care package you hand out to women like me? Like Tanya."

Something flickered through his eyes and she knew she'd struck home. Her gaze faltered as he took a step closer. Too close.

"What is it you want from me, Trey?"

"I want—" He stared at her, warring emotions sparking in his eyes, fighting their way to the surface as he searched for words.

She placed her hands on her hips and took a step to close the remaining distance between them. "Spit it out, Cowboy."

"I want—" He took a breath, his gaze locked on hers. "I want you to stay in Canyon Springs, Kara. Stay here. Call this home. Not Chicago."

Her mouth went dry. She hadn't expected that. Not anything like that. What was he saying? That he cared for her more than as a friend?

"Why?" she whispered.

He paused, indecision in his eyes. Then without warning he gently captured her face in his hands. "This is why."

Before she could react, he closed his eyes and leaned in. Lips parting, poised a mere breath away from her own as if waiting for permission.

Without hesitation, her lips met his. The barest whisper of a touch. With a breathless sigh, she gave in to the kiss she was more than ready to share.

He wanted her to stay. With him.

Time stood still as she relaxed into the kiss. Saw in her mind's eye every one of her Chicago dreams drift out the window. But she didn't care. Nothing else mattered but this moment right now. Twelve years in the making, coming home to Trey seemed so right. So inevitable. Her heart soared with hope. Possibilities.

New dreams she didn't even know she had. A home. A family.

Maybe God did have a few good surprises in store for her after all?

When at long last the kiss ended and Trey drew back, she looked shyly into his face, expecting to see the same revelation in his own eyes. The same dreams. The same giddy sense of wonder.

The same love.

The hands that had so gently cupped her face now moved to her waist, but he didn't meet her gaze.

With an uncertain smile, she reached up to touch his cheek. Felt the stubble along his strong jaw. "Wow, Cowboy. That's a mighty persuasive argument."

She wet her lips. Closed her eyes and tilted her head to brush her mouth softly against his once more. But he didn't respond.

"Trey?"

He finally looked at her. Eyes filled with pain. Regret.

She swallowed the lump forming in her throat. "Tell me what's wrong."

"I'm not sure I can."

"So what *was* this to you?" Her words came softly, but with an edge. "Another feel-good moment? Or a way to take back control? To shut me up about my dad?"

He glanced away again and she pried his warm fingers from her waist. Stepped back.

"We've kissed three times in our life, Cowboy—

twice in the last week. And every single time you stomp on the brake and shift into reverse. That Tanya woman must have really done a number on you."

Then the truth dawned. "Or couldn't you make a commitment to her either?"

"Kara—" He reached out his hand.

She backed away, her eyes boring into his. "Thanks for the invitation to make this town my home. But you know, Trey, I think it's best I do leave Canyon Springs. Staying here wouldn't do either of us any favors. And for a split second you almost made me forget something very important. I have a dream— and Canyon Springs isn't it."

Chapter Eighteen

The humiliation of those moments with Trey washed through Kara the next morning as she pulled sweaters from the dresser drawers and threw them on the bed. She wasn't in the mood to fold them so they could join everything else she'd crammed into the two open suitcases on the floor.

How could Trey show so much concern for her? Take such good care of her and kiss her like that— only to crawl back in his tight-lipped man cave and act like nothing had happened between them? And how on earth, for those few fleeting moments of insanity, had she tossed away her forever dreams and embraced racing back to Canyon Springs? All because some good-lookin' cowboy knew how to kiss.

She shoved the drawer closed. Trey couldn't make a commitment if his life depended on it. He said he wanted her to stay in town. Make Canyon Springs her home. But why? Let's hear it, mister. Silly her, for a few lunacy-ridden minutes she'd actually let herself believe it might be for a little more reason than that she was a good typist. Met deadlines. Made a good cup of coffee.

Mom was right. Cowboys were nothing but trouble.

"Packin' up, doll?"

She glanced up at her mother leaning on her walker in the doorway. Her coloring was much better now, her eyes brighter, voice stronger.

"Sorry I woke you up."

"You didn't wake me up. Wide awake. Thinkin' about things."

Kara sighed. "You know if I could do this any other way, I would. But you can't stay by yourself just yet. Aunt Tammy's is the best option. Hopefully we can get you resettled when I come for Meg's wedding in March."

Her mother waved her off. "That's not what I've been thinking about. Visiting my sister will be good for body and soul. Never could get away from the Warehouse often enough to do that."

"What's bothering you then?"

Mom moved in closer to the bed. Leaned over the walker to snag a sweater. "You. And that cowboy."

Kara broke eye contact with her mother. "Go ahead. Say 'I told you so.' I should have listened when you warned me about cowboys. You'd think I'd have gotten a clue after Dad."

"I was wrong about that, doll. It's you I should have been warning *Trey* about."

Kara stared at her mother.

"That day he had lunch here with the girls, I should have given him a heads-up. Let him know you were running so fast, so hard, to get out of Canyon Springs that he'd be left sittin' in the dust."

Kara gave a short laugh. "I'd stay, Mom, if he'd give me a reason to stay."

"That's what you're telling yourself?"

"If he had any feelings for me, he'd have told me. Trey Kenton's never been shy about speaking his mind."

Her mother scoffed. "But what about speaking his heart?"

"Believe me, he's had plenty of opportunities to verbalize it." Like when he crowded in close last evening for a kiss that still made her heart quiver. "Mom, I know how much it would mean to you, but I'm not coming back to Canyon Springs on a permanent basis. And certainly not with Trey. He has his own issues. I have mine. I have dreams, and I'm not going to come back here and rot for the rest of my life waiting for him to get around to 'speaking his heart.'"

"I know you have your dreams, doll. And none of them involve Canyon Springs."

Kara wadded up a sweater and tossed it at an open suitcase. "You grew up here, too, so it's hard for you to understand. But it's like my whole life is an open book in this town. I mean, this is a place where everyone remembers which kid threw up on the first day of kindergarten or got caught making out in the church parking lot or fumbled the ball two seconds before the homecoming game ended—even if that 'kid' is now fifty years old. People remember it like it happened yesterday. Nobody gets to grow up. Reinvent themselves. This is a town where everyone knows—"

"Whose dad botched a business deal that cost friends thousands, then ran off and left her and her mom?"

Kara drew in a sharp breath. "It wasn't easy, Mom."

"No, it wasn't. Still isn't. But you gotta forgive him, doll." Kara's jaw hardened. "I've heard this same song and dance from Trey, thank you."

"The boy's right. If you can't find it in your heart to forgive your dad, you can't be happy inside yourself. And if you can't be happy inside yourself, chances are you won't find happiness anywhere else either. Not here, not Chicago."

"Maybe you can forgive and forget, but I can't."

"Forgiving and forgetting are two different things. I haven't forgotten. But with God's help I choose to forgive—not in the past tense 'chose,' but in an active, continuing tense. Not because it's letting your dad off the hook but because it would destroy my life if I let it. Like you're letting it destroy yours."

"My life hasn't been destroyed."

"Maybe not instantaneously like an imploding building, but you're letting this chip away at your happiness. Allowing it to color your decision making.

Cast a shadow over your future. Push that fine young man away."

"I didn't push him away, Mom. Trey and I—we're just not meant to be."

"My, my, doesn't that sound noble."

"Mom, please, I don't want to remember our last day together like this. That we argued."

"Sorry to burst your bubble, but relationships can be messy. You can't keep avoiding life, running away."

"They say you can't go home again, and Trey and I proved it. Coming back here didn't do anything for either of us but open up old wounds."

"Sometimes you have to open up a wound to let the infection drain. Allow it to heal over, to leave a scar that gradually fades away. But you can't keep picking at the scab. Talking about it. Dwelling on it. Opening it up again and again. Which is exactly what you've done with your dad."

"Mom, *please?* You and I have come so far since I was a teenager. The relationship we've developed means so much to me. Don't let Dad and Trey ruin what we've found together."

"I want you to be happy, doll."

"I know." Kara stepped forward and pulled her mother into a warm embrace. "Don't worry, Mom, I will be. Just as soon as I can get out of here."

I have a dream and Canyon Springs isn't it.

If he wanted a sign from God that the door had closed, you couldn't get much clearer than Kara's own words. She was a city girl through and through now. Didn't want any part of small-town life. Or him. But if she'd have stuck around another day or two, maybe he'd have gathered the courage to risk a slap to the face for kissing her on Valentine's Day. Like Mary insisted was the key.

Followed by Rowdy, he slipped into a box stall where Taco rummaged for the last remnants of his Monday morning breakfast in the bucket anchored to the wall.

"You're thinkin' I could have stopped her, aren't you, old boy?" The horse leaned his head into Trey, looking to have the sweet spot behind his ear scratched. "You're thinkin' I should have told her. You know, that I…love her."

There, he'd said it out loud.

Taco stomped a hoof and heaved a contented sigh.

"You're thinkin' that's why she left, aren't you? Because I couldn't say it." He brushed his fingers through the coarse hairs of the horse's mane. "But I can't. Not with her acting the way she is about her dad. Blaming God for everything. Not believing I can keep a commitment—just like Tanya."

But could he keep a commitment? He'd long asked himself that. Had he used all the years of transient living as an excuse to keep his heart at a distance? Always moved on when he started to get too close. Before expectations of a long-term relationship were raised. Tanya had stuck around two years before giving up on him. Looking back, he probably *had* been a jerk. Should have been up-front with her to begin with about his reservations about them. But it had been good to have someone to hang out with. Not always having to do things on your own. Alone. And it's not like he didn't care for Tanya. He did. But why hadn't he fallen in love with her?

Was it because of Kara?

He looked out the open portion of the half door leading to an adjacent paddock. In the dim morning light the moon hung between the clouds in the western sky, casting shadows on the frozen white ground.

As always when he looked up at the craggy, illuminated orb, he couldn't help but be aware that was the very same moon Jesus had gazed up at two thousand years ago. A comforting connection. And the same moon that shone on him now would be gazing down on Kara in Chicago tomorrow night.

A little tune played through his memory. One his mom used to sing to him when he was a tyke. About how the moon could "see" somebody you yourself would like to see. He hummed the few bars he could remember, then rubbed the back of his neck.

What he'd give to see Kara every day for the rest of his life. To hold her in his arms. To whisper his love in her ear. To take care of her. Share his life with her. But God—and Kara—had a different plan. So there was no point in kickin' at the traces. Fightin' the bit.

Why'd he have to go and fall for her all over again?

But sure as shootin' he had. As easy as a calf jumpin' over a caterpillar. And all the while his common sense kept hauling on the reins, trying to get him to pull up, but he kept on going.

He glanced again at the moon, then shook his head. Gave Taco a pat. "Besides, what's the use in sayin' anything about love to her? I'm not movin' to Chicago. And if you'd have heard her, you'd know wild horses couldn't drag her back here."

No, there wasn't anything he could do it about it. It was what it was. God closed the door.

But he could still lend her a hand. Make things easier for her to pursue her dream. And he knew just the person who could help him do it.

"I see a member of our team has returned at long last," Garson Design's Gabrielle Dubois announced with a condescending smile at Kara. The department head stood overlooking the gathering in the main conference room. "Welcome back, Kara—from ridin' and ropin' or whatever else it is you cowgirl types do in your spare time."

The mocking words stung.

"Yee haw," someone in the back of the room said quietly. But everyone heard it. Snickered.

Kara sent Spence a questioning glance. He returned it with a thin smile. Betrayed. By the one person she thought she could count on at Garson.

"Actually, ma'am," Kara said with an exaggerated

drawl. "Spare time's spent pickin' out the best chewin' tabaccer money can buy."

Everyone laughed. With her. Not at her.

So there, Gabrielle.

Spence.

But a queasiness in her stomach persisted as the meeting settled into its usual routine. She looked around the room filled with the familiar faces of those she'd worked with for almost five years. Served together on teams. Faced mutual challenges. Celebrated accomplishments. But if she walked out the door right now, would she miss any of them?

The soaring ceiling with open ductwork caught her eye. A sweep of angled windows. Recessed lighting. Bold, colorful artwork. A design studio on the cutting edge. How it had thrilled her twenty-two-year-old heart when she'd come to do a preprofessional residency the summer between her junior and senior year of college. And how unbelievable when postgraduation she'd been invited to interview. Electrifying to be hired right into the heart of the Chicago design world.

But how could the heartbeat of the company that once had her dancing to its rhythm suddenly no longer appeal? She'd been gone a few months, yet no one asked about her mother's health that morning. Or said they missed her. It was almost as if she'd never been gone. But that's what she'd always liked about Garson Design, wasn't it? Everyone focused on the moment.

No one knew her past, stereotyped her. She could be anyone here she wanted to be.

Until Spence told someone about her cowboy dad.

She'd been labeled now. No longer sophisticated metro Phoenix, but cowboy's daughter. Hick. She'd been careful to keep up an urbane image. The clothes. The shoes. The hair. The nails. She'd eliminated conversational references to screaming deals at Walmart and her love affair with pickups. Watched her diction and guarded against regional colloquialisms—although she'd slipped back into those recently.

She sat up straighter. She was the same designer this week that she was before she left for Canyon Springs at Thanksgiving. She could still do the job. Clients would still like and respect her. Maybe she could use the cowgirl slant to her advantage. Like a product "brand." Play up Arizona. The West.

After all, her future was wide open now. Nothing to tie her down to Canyon Springs. For as much as she resented her mother mentioning the situation to him, Dad stepped in with a loan. Called Mom at Aunt Tammy's house Monday afternoon. But although she may now be indebted to her father financially, you couldn't buy someone's love. Or forgiveness.

Even as she mentally pumped herself up with thoughts of a Garson Design future, however, memory flashed to the day she'd worked out Taco as Trey watched. The clank of the bit, the squeak of leather, rhythmic hoofbeats. Trey's satisfied grin and a tip of his hat as she rode back toward him.

With effort, she refocused on Gabrielle, but as the team leader droned on about the conditions leading to recent layoffs, Kara glanced up at the clock—11:00 a.m. Ten o'clock in Arizona. Had Trey stopped in for his morning coffee after he'd completed his chores? Had a little chat with cousin Brielle? Or now that Kara wasn't there, would he drift over to Camilla's? Or Kit's? Or replace the defunct coffeepot in his office?

Was Brielle getting the hang of things at the Warehouse? Had Sandi found anyone to help out with the housing project? Did Mary like the pillowcases? Had Trey made up his mind if he'd stay in Canyon Springs or not?

Their last meeting had ended on a bad note. She still resented his shallow kiss. His deception about her dad. But maybe she should call him. Assure him she was settling back into Chicago life. Let him know that while awaiting her flight at Sky Harbor she'd found cute hair accessories for Mary in one of the shops.

"—and in conclusion," Gabrielle continued, "I think we all recognize that tough times call for even tougher measures, more focused attitudes. A willingness to invest the extra time and effort that will keep Garson Design in the game."

Kara joined in the light smattering of applause.

Yes, she'd call Trey tonight.

Chapter Nineteen

Trey checked the caller ID of his ringing cell phone.

Kara.

With renewed determination, he let it go to messaging and added another piece to the puzzle he and Mary were putting together on the Warehouse apartment dining table. He glanced over at Missy playing quietly with her dolls on a corner of the sofa, talking animatedly to herself.

Kara had called twice that week. Once on Wednesday night to tell him she was safely in the Windy City and that she'd found hair doodads for Mary. Was sending them priority mail. Then Thursday she called to ask if he could give her Reyna's cell phone number.

Now it was Saturday night. He'd finished up at the equine center. Showered. Flopped on the sofa, too tired to even turn on the TV while he'd awaited the arrival of his nieces. He'd volunteered early in the week to give Jason and Reyna a date night without the girls—one of those things Jason's premarital guides recommended. At least the prior commitment gave him a good excuse to dodge an unanticipated volley of demands on his free time.

A single gal at the church had invited him to a dinner gathering at her place, but he'd begged off. And another of Meg's friends, Samantha Couldn't-Remember-Her-Last-Name, called to remind him of a moonlight cross-country ski outing with other singles from a sister church in Pinetop-Lakeside. He turned down that one, too. Sure seemed with Kara gone that the unattached ladies of Canyon Springs had come out in droves.

Is that what life would be like if he settled down here permanently? Not that the attention wasn't flattering, but he'd rather be hanging out with Kara. Listening to her talk. Watching the sway of her ponytail down her back. How her gray eyes sparkled when amused—or flashed when she was really into something. Like giving him what for.

Rather be remembering how her soft lips tasted on his.

Which didn't exactly explain why he'd let the phone go to messaging instead of picking up.

"It's your turn, Uncle Trey."

"Oh, sorry." He selected a colorful piece of shaped cardboard and slid it into place.

"That's not where it goes. That's an eye."

"It fits."

"No it doesn't." She shoved the piece back at him.

"Are you tired, princess?" She hadn't been her usual perky self tonight. Maybe she was coming down with something. "Ready for bed?"

She gave him a dirty look. "No."

He reached across the table and put his hand on her forehead. She jerked back.

"I just want to see if you have a fever."

"I'm not sick."

"Then what's the problem?"

With an obstinate jut of her chin, she folded her arms. "It's your fault Kara left. You didn't kiss her on Valemtime's Day."

Oh, boy.

"Kissing doesn't always make everything right, Mary." He should know. And if Kara kept calling and he kept answering, he'd never get over her. Never be ready to see what God had in store for him next.

Not that he had much interest in a love life right now.

With the High Country Equine Center set to launch in a couple of months—he was still determined to get that final approval from Reuben Falkner—his goal was nearly met. But without the extra cash he'd saved up it would be hard, if not impossible, to embark on and promote his long dreamed of horse training venture on the side.

But he'd figure out a way to do it. One of these days. If he ever felt like it.

"If you'd have kissed her, she would have stayed." Mary's cheerless tone echoed his own unenthusiastic thoughts. "Are you going to stay, Uncle Trey?"

Was he? He stared down at the now-silent cell phone on the table. "I don't know, Mary."

"But you've got to." Her lower lip protruded.

You're not making this easy on me, God.

Even before Kara had returned at Thanksgiving, he'd sensed her presence in her hometown. Had known better than to come back to Canyon Springs. But once he was spending time with family—with Missy and Mary—he'd convinced himself he could make a go of it. That old memories would be overlaid with new ones. That he'd clear his name, find himself a nice hometown girl and start his dreamed-of family.

But he'd been wrong. Kara had come back just long enough to lasso his heart, throw it to the ground and tie it up with a pigg'n string.

Again.

Mary stood up. "I don't want to do a puzzle anymore."

He wasn't much in the mood for it either. "Then come here and give me a hug."

He knew she was mad at him. Saw her hesitation. The war going on within. Then her ever-soft heart won out and she came around the table to wrap her arms around his neck. Man, did he love this little girl.

Wanted to make her happy. Wanted to be there for her. But—

When she pulled back, her dark solemn eyes gazed into his. "You should have kissed her, Uncle Trey."

She patted his leg, then all but dragging her feet she moved off to join Missy on the sofa. Her body language spelled out a heaviness in her heart that rivaled his.

He glanced again at the cell phone.

Guess he'd better see what Kara had to say. Make sure there hadn't been an emergency. Something he needed to take care of for her. He retrieved the message.

"Um, hi, Trey. It's me," the familiar voice began, her tone light and lilting. "Nine o'clock Chicago time. Eight o'clock Canyon Springs. Guess you're working late tonight. No rest for the wicked, huh? Or maybe you're out on a hot date?"

A soft giggle warmed his heart. But she'd guessed wrong. There was only one woman with whom he was interested in sharing a hot date.

"Anyway," she continued, "I just thought I'd check in and see how things went at the meeting with old Reuben yesterday. Well, guess that's all for now. Bye."

He listened to the message two more times, then placed the phone back on the table. Slid back in his chair, stretched his legs out. Bumped Rowdy curled sleeping at his feet.

No, things hadn't gone well with "Old Reuben."

He wouldn't return Kara's call tonight. Didn't feel like talking about the councilman's continued insinuations about his past. He'd text her tomorrow. Let her know how things stood. But could she be lonely? Missing home? Him? Was that why she'd called three times since returning to her dream world?

Naw. She was where she wanted to be. Probably just felt sorry for him. *Dumb old cowboy, thinking you could win her heart. Be enough to keep her from going back to Chicago.*

Maybe he could have if he'd spoken up? *Kissed her on Valemtime's Day?* But after Tanya he'd promised God he wouldn't get involved with a woman who didn't put a lot of stock in faith issues. Who didn't share his beliefs.

Or was he hesitating because of what she'd done to him as a teen? Didn't quite trust her for letting him take the fall for something she knew he hadn't done. Had he forgiven her as he'd told her he had? Or did that still stand between them?

Whatever the answer, it was a moot point. An old cowpoke like him couldn't keep her happy in Canyon Springs. And he sure as shootin' couldn't be an urban cowboy. So where'd that leave them? Same place they'd been since the first night they ran into each other outside Kit's Lodge.

Worlds apart.

Kara leaned her forehead against the cool window of the darkened apartment, gazing down at the street far below. Bumper-to-bumper traffic. Headlights and streetlights. Glowing neon signs and lit windows of other apartments across the way.

How could you be sitting in the middle of a teeming city of millions and feel so all alone?

She'd been back three weeks now. Three long weeks. Her roommates were out for the evening again and she had the place to herself. Time to think without interruption. To celebrate her freedom far from the confines of Canyon Springs.

But Trey hadn't returned her recent calls. Any of them. He did send a brief text message telling her things remained hung up with Lindi's grandpa. Which only made her feel worse. His business wouldn't have hit a logjam if she'd defied Lindi and just told him the truth.

Why should she be surprised, though, that he'd texted and not called? She'd lit into him but good about knowing her dad and keeping it a secret from her. Questioned his honesty, his integrity—two things he was ultrasensitive about because of the low-down thing she'd done to him as a teen. What a hypocrite she was. While it angered her, the promise he'd made to her dad didn't come close to the one she'd made to Lindi. His offense paled in comparison to hers.

But still, he'd kissed her, hadn't he? Even after she argued with him about her dad. He said he wanted her to stay in Canyon Springs. But of course, he couldn't come up with a good reason—the only reason that could have changed her mind about what she did with her future.

Nevertheless, she'd called a couple of times. An excuse, really, to hear his voice, sort of smooth things over. He'd been polite, but not talkative. Then he'd stopped picking up on her calls. She'd left a few messages, then took the hint—didn't call even to tell him she'd been giving thought to what he'd said about forgiving her father.

Even praying about it.

After all, what else was there to do when you came home to an empty apartment? Oh, sure, she could have gone out with the after-work office crowd. Joined her roommates at a trendy nightspot. But after a few evenings of that the first week, the crowds, the noise, it seemed so pointless. Artificial. Forcing herself to smile. Laugh. Pretending to have a good time when all she wanted was to slip off for a quiet walk under the stars. Preferably with Trey.

She stared out the apartment window at the sky above, but couldn't even see any stars from here. At least she glimpsed what might be the moon overhead, rising above the buildings down the street. But it seemed more hazy and far away than it did back home.

With a sigh she drew a finger across the cold plate of window glass. This was just a phase she was going through, right? An adjustment period before she got back into the swing of things. She'd gotten too used to her sleepy hometown the past few months. To seeing people she knew on the street, in the shops and restaurants. At church. People asking how she was. Chatting about old times. Hoping she'd come back.

Now she found herself missing the fresh pine air. The brilliance of a high country Arizona sky. Mom's laughter. Meg's friendship. Mary and Missy's giggles.

Trey's smile.

Seems to me that most people can be about as happy as they make up their minds to be, no matter where they live.

Could he be right? Mom seemed to think so. Was it something she could just make up her mind about? Could she be happy in Canyon Springs by *deciding* she would be? If she turned her life back over to God—stopped dredging up the past, replaying it in her mind, repeating it with her mouth—would the pain of her father's abandonment gradually fade away? Could the past, tied so closely to Canyon Springs, stop overshadowing her future if she trusted God to make it happen?

She needed to think more on this one. Pray. Forgiving her father, though, seemed minor compared to the other obstacle to her happiness. She stared out the window for several more minutes. Then picked up the cell phone from where she'd placed it on the upholstered arm of the chair. She had to tell Trey the truth.

But how would she convince Lindi, who'd been so opposed?

Nevertheless, for the hundredth time since they'd breakfasted together at Kit's, she punched in the speed dial for Lindi's number.

And listened to it ring.

Chapter Twenty

Kara headed to the rental car she'd parked in back of Mom's house an hour ago. She'd flown into Phoenix early that morning, then picked up her mother in Prescott and was now headed to the Friday night wedding rehearsal for Meg and Joe.

Thank goodness the weather looked to be perfect for her friend's special weekend. Sunny and temps almost to fifty. March, traditionally a big snow month in mountain country, could make for dicey travel conditions. But even though a layer of snow still piled one to two feet deep in unmelted shady spots, the roads were clear and dry where sunlight warmed the pavement.

She glanced over at the garage, paused, then took a few more steps toward the rental car. Paused again. Mom still kept Dad's old Mustang in drivable condition. Even drove it when she wasn't in need of the SUV's hauling capacity or the weather didn't require four-wheel drive.

She took another hesitant step, then abruptly changed direction. Strode to the garage and let herself in the side door. Flipped a switch on the wall. The cream-colored Mustang shone in the bare-bulb illumination of the overhead light.

She stood undecided for a moment, then approached to run a gloved hand along the glossy hood. Dad's pride and joy. How she used to love to go riding in it, around town or out in the country with the windows rolled down. They'd always stopped for an ice cream cone in the summertime. Her, Mom, Dad. Back when they were a family.

The Mustang's paperwork was in her name. Why hadn't she sold it before now?

She opened the driver's side door, retrieved the keys from where Mom always left them in the ignition, then opened up the trunk. Even in the dim light she confirmed the translucent, plastic bin was still wedged in the back corner where she'd left it. Filled with unread cards and letters from Dad. For whatever reason, even in her most angry and anguished moments as a teen, she hadn't the heart to tear them up and throw them away.

Maybe she'd get them out this weekend. Read them. It would be a start. After all, she'd told God on the flight to Phoenix that not only was she coming home to Canyon Springs for a wedding, but she was coming home to Him on a permanent basis.

Moved by a sudden impulse, she shut the trunk, tossed her purse to the passenger seat, then slid in behind the wheel. Pulled the door shut. Fastened the seat belt. She reached up to the remote control clipped to the sun visor, pressed the button and heard the garage door rise on its tracks.

Closing her eyes for a brief moment, she turned the key in the ignition. The engine jumped to life, and with an unexpected sense of liberation she carefully backed the car out.

So far so good.

With each block she drove to the church, the car's engine humming, a weight lifted from her shoulders. And by the time she pulled into the parking lot, she'd come to a decision.

She'd call and talk to Dad.

Of course, that was assuming he still wanted to hear from her. She'd spent the past fifteen years keeping him out of her life. Told him he'd made his decision to walk out on her and he could just live with it. She'd refused his calls. His correspondence. Had hidden out at Reyna's house when he'd shown up out of the blue on her sixteenth birthday. She must have finally made her point. He hadn't attempted to contact her in person since then.

She still wasn't sure how much she wanted him back in her life now. Maybe not much. But she wouldn't slam any doors.

All thoughts of her father, however, flew out the window as she stood at the front of the church watching Meg almost float down the aisle on a wave of happiness. Clad in jeans and a tunic sweater, but carrying a paper plate plastered with ribbons and bows, she looked every bit as beautiful as she would the following day. With a pang of melancholy, Kara couldn't help but notice how from the front of the church Joe's warm, loving gaze locked on his bride to be.

What would it be like to have a man look at you that way? To see your faults, know your weaknesses, yet have the courage to commit to you for a lifetime? Would she ever experience that for herself? And would she ever want the man waiting for her at the front of the church to be anyone other than Trey Kenton?

You're such a ninny, Kara.

She'd glimpsed him seated in one of the back rows—Meg had asked him to serve as an usher seating guests—but she kept her attention focused on the bride and groom. On Davy the cute ring bearer. Giggling flower girls Missy and Mary. Listened to the teasing, encouraging words shared by the minister, Jason Kenton. Before she knew it, she was trailing the couple back down the aisle to the fellowship hall for the rehearsal dinner.

Repeatedly throughout the dinner and festive celebration, she'd start to approach Trey, only to have someone else pull him aside for a few words. Missy or Mary often drew near him for a hug or to be picked up. Over and over she herself got sidetracked for informal pictures and "welcome home" conversations with longtime friends.

And then she saw her. Lindi. Crossing from an

outside entrance into the kitchen adjoining the meeting hall, a metal warming tray in her mittened hands. She was catering the event? Her cousin had evaded her for weeks. But tonight Kara would have some answers.

To her relief, the kitchen was empty except for Lindi. The handful of teenage waiters and waitresses were busy with their duties in the fellowship hall. She slipped inside and closed the sliding door.

Lindi turned. "I was hoping you'd find me here."

"Where have you been? I've called you for weeks and weeks. Texted. Left messages."

"I was mad at you."

"No kidding."

"I don't want to argue, Kara."

"Neither do I. But you need to know I'm going to tell Trey the truth tonight, no matter what you say. Your grandfather is refusing to sign the final papers for Trey to launch his business. Blames him for the fire. I can't allow that. I can't continue to live this lie."

Lindi's words came barely above a whisper. "Neither can I."

Had she heard right? Was this an answered prayer—or wishful thinking?

"You asked where I've been." Lindi adjusted the lid of a warming tray. "Avoiding you, to begin with. But the past two weeks James and I've been in California. In intensive marriage counseling. Got back yesterday."

"Counseling? You're working things out?"

"I think so. But we still have a long way to go." She rinsed off her hands in the sink, then dried them on a dish towel and looked Kara in the eye. "I, um, told him about the fire."

"And?"

"He's the only person I've ever told besides you. He was shocked, of course, but says he'll stand by me."

"Thank God."

"It was…freeing. We plan to move to Phoenix. Together. Surprised?" She laughed, then sobered. "Last night I told Grandpa about us moving and it didn't go over well. But I've come to realize what a chokehold on my life maintaining this lie has been. Not only how wrong of me it was to allow Trey to take the fall for something I did, but for me to hold you to that promise."

"So I do have your permission to tell him?"

She nodded. "I ran into Trey yesterday afternoon. Asked him if he'd talked to you recently. If he knew when you'd be getting back for the wedding. Within minutes, I knew he was one miserable man—without you. It was as if blinders had come off my eyes and I could finally see clearly that my lying, and my forcing you to lie, had possibly cost you the love of your life. I'm so sorry, Kara. Can you ever forgive me?"

How could she not, when she so badly needed to be forgiven herself? She hurried to her cousin's side and pulled her into a hug.

"I need to talk to Trey," Lindi said, holding her tight. "But I wanted to tell you first."

"And I want to talk to Trey before you do. Apologizing of my own is in order."

Lindi gave her another hug. "On Monday, let's go see my grandpa, okay? Tell him the truth. Get him to sign those papers."

"Thank you, Lindi."

And thank you, God.

It had been a long evening, beginning with watching from the back row of the church as the ponytailed Kara had walked up the aisle to await Meg's arrival. How'd she keep getting more and more beautiful? And how'd he ever think not returning her calls would be a cure for his…heart problem?

He now leaned against the door of his pickup in a darkened corner of the parking lot and stared up at the full moon rising in the eastern sky. Had it been a month since he'd seen her? A month since he'd kissed her?

Man, why couldn't he get that out of his head?

With Sharon Dixon in Prescott, he hadn't heard any updates on how things were going in Chicago. Except, of course, for the calls he'd gotten from Kara herself that first week after she'd left. The calls he didn't return. As he'd intended, his lack of response put a halt to her attempts to contact him. So why'd he still persist in getting his hopes up each time he checked his messages? Set himself up for disappointment?

You'd have thought she'd at least have spoken to him tonight. But she appeared all caught up in the excitement of the eve of Meg and Joe's wedding. Into the moment. Focusing on her maid of honor duties. Enjoying chatting with old friends.

Or rather, *some* old friends.

Not him.

With a heavy sigh, he unlocked the pickup door and climbed in. Started the engine.

He couldn't go through this every time Kara came back for a visit. It had been a hard lesson to learn, but he'd finally come to the right decision.

To leave Canyon Springs.

Chapter Twenty-One

Trey was nowhere to be found.

In desperation, Kara slipped away from the festivities, out a side door and into the stillness of the night. As was typical of the high country in March, the night air was cold and clear. Stars sparkled overhead, the moon's face glowed low on the horizon, barely filtering through the trees. Even with the fixture over the door and a single streetlamp lighting the parking lot, it was too dark to tell if Trey's truck was still there. She suspected he'd left.

But he'd have to come back for the wedding tomorrow, wouldn't he?

She leaned against a post by the side door and gazed up into the moon-silhouetted pines. Only a month ago she'd said her goodbyes to Canyon Springs. Goodbyes to the dreams that were never to be. Maybe it was just as well that Trey hadn't lingered tonight, that she hadn't caught up with him. How could she face him without making a fool of herself? Without letting him see the humiliating truth that she cared for him far more than he'd ever cared for her?

How could she look him in the eye and tell him that she'd known all this time who started the fire? Had let him pay the price for it?

But that's what she had to do. Would do. Tomorrow.

"Kara?"

A distinctive male voice spoke from the darkness. Her breath caught. She momentarily closed her eyes, turning to grip the support post to steady herself. She hadn't anticipated this. Hadn't prepared herself.

"Dad?"

A tall man emerged from the shadows and slowly approached, his familiar rolling gait confirming her recognition of the gravelly voice. The dim light illuminated his Western felt hat and suede jacket, the craggy features of his face. He had to be pushing sixty now, but she'd have known him anywhere.

"What are you doing here?" she said softly, her mind still not comprehending that the man she hadn't wanted anything to do with since she was thirteen stood before her. Had he driven all the way from New Mexico to see her? Or happened to be in the neighborhood on equine center business?

"Your mom said you were comin' back for a wedding." He pulled the hat from his head and clutched it in front of him with both hands, like a schoolboy called on the carpet. "I know you never wanted to see me again. You have every reason in the world not to. I brought a shame down on my family that still grieves me. That's why I didn't have the heart to demand shared custody. Visitation rights. But—"

"Dad—"

"Saw the Mustang." He jerked his head toward the parking lot.

She hugged her arms to herself, both to keep warm and to stop her hands from shaking. "Drives pretty good."

He gave what sounded like a relieved chuckle. "Does it?"

"Mmm-hmm."

Both stared, drinking in the presence of the other as if coming across a stream in a water-parched land.

A numbness seeped in around her heart.

Dad. He was here.

"I, uh, don't want to keep you from your wedding responsibilities. Know you have lots going on tonight." He shifted his weight, glanced at the ground, then back at her. "But when I saw the car, I thought if I waited long enough maybe I'd catch a glimpse of you. And when you stepped out with that long ponytail, I knew it was you—all beautiful and grown up. I couldn't hang back. I mean, just look at you. The spittin' image of your mother when she was your age."

"Dad—"

"I couldn't wait one more day to tell you how sorry I am for what I did to you. To your mom."

"Dad—"

"I've no excuses. Not one. I can't go back and

change anything. I can't erase the pain. I can't make it up to you. But I want you to know—" His voice cracked. "Know I'm sorry. And that I love you, little girl."

He held open his arms.

She hesitated. Did he think he could walk back into her life as easy as you please, just like he walked out? That he could pick up where they left off and she'd be good with it? That he only had to—

And forgive us our trespasses as we forgive those who trespass against us.

The words of the Lord's Prayer she'd memorized as a child pierced her conscience. She needed Trey to forgive her. *As we forgive…*

A whimper escaped her lips. "Oh, Dad, I'm so sorry. I love you, too."

She stepped into his welcoming embrace. The smell of leather. His familiar aftershave. Stepped back into time. Time before he left. Time before she'd hardened her heart against him, built a protective shell to keep him out.

They stood together for some time, his calloused hand patting her hair. Her soaking his jacket front with tears.

"Trey was right," he said at long last, his voice not yet steady. "He said it was time. Said we needed each other."

She pulled back and he handed her a handkerchief. "I forgot. You know Trey."

"Known him since he was in college, cuttin' his

teeth on rodeoin' in the summer." He chuckled. "He said you were madder at him than a bull on a rampage for not telling you he was working with me."

She dabbed at her eyes. "I let him have it, that's for sure." He chuckled again. "That's my girl. Don't let him get away with anything."

He scuffed a booted toe at the ground, his next words spoken in a more serious tone. "But don't place the blame on him, missy. That was my doing. I made him promise not to say anything to anyone in Canyon Springs long before you showed up to take care of your mother."

So Trey hadn't lied about that.

"That young man thinks the world of you, little girl."

A wistful sigh escaped her lips. "Don't I wish."

He gripped her arm and gave it a light shake. "Hey, now, what's it take for a young buck to get your attention? Giving up his own dream isn't enough?"

She crumpled the handkerchief in her hand. "What do you mean?"

"He loaned your mom the money to pay off her medical bills. That's a pretty clear marker of serious interest in my book."

"He offered to pay the bills," she clarified, "but I turned him down. You paid them off."

"Who do you think gave me the money? Handed over his nest egg so you wouldn't be under pressure when you headed back to the big city."

Her grip tightened on the handkerchief. "What?"

"He didn't want you or your mom to know. But after seein' him moping around today like a stray in search of the herd—and puttin' two and two together and comin' up with *you*—I can't keep my mouth shut."

She stared at him, trying to take in everything he'd said. "You're serious, aren't you?"

"Sure am. Just as sure as I'm standing here and you're standing there with that same dumbfounded look you used to get on your face as a kid when someone pulled a fast one on you."

"I don't understand. Why would Trey give you money to loan me and Mom?"

"I told you." He lightly pecked his index finger on her forehead. "He's head over heels in L-O-V-E. All I can say is you'd better wake up and smell the coffee, 'cause soon as he finds another property manager to take over our project, he's lightin' out of here."

"No, he'll find a way to stay in Canyon Springs. He wants to be near family. His nieces."

"Could if he wanted to, I suppose. But it looks like he can't stomach the place without you."

She gripped her dad's arm to steady herself.

"Do you have feelings for him, Kara?"

"I—" She stared into her father's eyes but it was Trey who filled her mind. Her heart. Trey whom she'd betrayed. Trey who'd forgiven her for what he thought she'd done to him. Trey who'd supported her, encouraged her. Who enabled her to return to Chicago with

Mom's medical bills paid. Saved the Warehouse. "I think—I love him."

Her dad raised a brow. "Well, then?"

"It's not that simple, Dad. There's so much you don't know. So much no one knows. Not even Trey."

"I don't know what you're frettin' about, sugar, but if you have any feelings for him at all, I'm thinkin' you'd better get a move on. You and I can talk later. Go on now, git!"

The apartment above the Warehouse was dark, but she hit the gas and cruised on through main street. Then past the glowing lights of residential neighborhoods and on toward the other side of town. Rounded a familiar curve and broke through the stand of trees where the still-frosty, burned-out acreage of Duffy's place stretched out in the moonlight.

Heart drumming, she slowed, searching for the iron-arched entrance. Turned the car up the drive. Said a prayer. No matter what happened when she saw Trey, when she made her confession, she'd drive back down the lane knowing she'd come clean. Broken free of the shackles of her twelve-year deception.

The indoor arena lights blazed, and she parked next to Trey's pickup. Then slipped inside. Drank in the smell of horses, grain and hay. Could hear the rhythm of shod hooves on the groomed floor of the arena. The squeak of leather. Rattle of a bit. A horse's snort.

Standing in the shadows, Rowdy brushing up against her leg, she watched in fascinated silence as

Trey put Beamer through his paces in the center of the arena. His expertise made her own feeble performance of a month ago fade in comparison. This man knew his stuff. Knew his horse. Would be a great trainer.

It was only when fifteen minutes later he stepped down from the saddle to lead Beamer back to the stable area that she made her presence known.

"Quite a ride, Cowboy."

His head jerked up and he stared, unseeing, in her direction, the arena lights blinding him to where she stood.

"Kara?"

She moved to the gate where he could see her, then opened it and slipped inside, Rowdy at her heels. Trey paused for a long moment, his expression uncertain, then turned Beamer in her direction and limped across the expanse toward her. She met him halfway, willing her heart to quiet.

Please, God, get me through this.

He came to a halt a few feet away, but Beamer stretched out a muscled neck, nostrils quivering, to check her out. She scratched the big bay under the chin. What to say? Where to start? "I saw Dad tonight."

"And?"

"And while I don't know what kind of relationship we'll have in the future, it's a start."

He nodded. "Glad to hear it."

"He said you told him it was time. And you were right."

"Could I get that in writing? Maybe in liquid gold?"

She heard the smile in his voice and returned it as she patted Beamer's neck. "You were right, too, about God being involved in my life all along. For fifteen years I've been so angry at Dad, at myself—and even at God—that I couldn't recognize it. Recognize Him. Until I had time alone this past month to rethink—pray—about a lot of things. Things you'd said. Mom. Things God's been saying to me for a long time and I refused to listen. Until now."

Trey nodded his understanding.

"God and I are on the same team again. I made a decision to forgive Dad. Now I need God to teach me how work it out in my heart. Through action. How to work through the roller-coaster emotions."

"It'll take time."

"Dad told me something else, too." She pinned her gaze on Trey. "That you gave him the money to loan to me and Mom."

His brows lowered as irritation flashed. "You weren't supposed to know that. He wasn't supposed to tell."

"Well, he did. So you can take that up with him." Beamer nibbled at the hem of her jacket and she gently pushed his head away. "But thank you. You shouldn't have done it, Trey. It's too much. I don't deserve it."

"I wanted to do it, Kara, or I wouldn't have."

She took a deep breath. "When I get back to Chicago, I'll get a second job. Get you paid off as fast as I can."

"No hurry. Take your time." He toyed with Beamer's reins. "So you're still determined to go back to Chicago."

"That's where my job is." She forced a smile. "If you'd like to see your money in this lifetime, you'd better hope I keep it."

"Your job's there. Is that where your heart is, too?"

Ever since Trey's return to town, she'd sang the praises of her life in the city. Her career. The promotion. The dream. Took every opportunity to put down the community she'd grown up in. Belittled his hope to settle here.

Was her heart still in Chicago?

"Not so much anymore." She glanced at the ground. "Ironic, isn't it? The past month I've been there has been quite an eye-opener. Small-town America is looking better and better."

He looped the near side stirrup over the saddle horn, then loosened Beamer's cinch, but didn't respond.

Guess that was that. Her lips tightened. "Well, I guess I'll see you tomorrow. At the wedding?"

"Right."

He continued to fiddle with the saddle. She turned away and with leaden legs headed back toward the gate. Dad had it all wrong. Trey wasn't head over heels for her. Never had been. Loaning the money had been one of the many do-gooder deeds of a man who couldn't make a long-term commitment if his life depended on it.

Loner. Tumbleweed.

With a jolt, she halted. Her business wasn't done here yet. Fortifying herself with another silent prayer, knowing what she was about to tell him would seal the distance between them forever, she turned.

And came face-to-face with Trey.

Chapter Twenty-Two

He'd startled her, his turning Beamer loose and coming up behind her like that. Just like the night at Meg's when he'd found her in the laundry room cleaning off soda cans. Gray eyes wide and beautiful.

He swallowed the lump in his throat, still not quite believing his own ears. What she'd just shared with him. That God had led her back home. To His heart.

Come on, Kenton. It's now or never.

"If you're no longer sold on Chicago, Kara," he spoke the words softly, reaching out to catch her hand in his, "why don't you stay in Canyon Springs—"

Her gaze met his uncertainly and he realized she'd heard that identical invitation before. The night they'd had their falling out because he couldn't—

Spit it out, Cowboy. Isn't that what she'd said?

He took a steadying breath. "Why don't you stay in Canyon Springs, Kara—with a man who loves you?"

The look sweeping across her face caught him off guard. Belted him squarely in the gut. He expected to see surprise. Maybe bewilderment. But not panic. Fear.

He loosened the grip on her hand, certain she'd feel the wave of cold coursing through his limbs. "I take it that's not what you wanted to hear."

She tightened her fingers on his, eyes pleading. "It's exactly what any woman would dream of hearing from you, Trey."

"Any woman." His voice sounded hollow, expressionless. "But not you."

"I'm sorry, Trey. I—"

"Don't be." His jaw hardened as he took a step back, but she held fast to his hands. If she'd let go of him, he'd put them both out of their misery, make himself scarce.

"Hear me out, Trey. Please? Your words—they're what I've dreamed of since I was sixteen years old. But I'm not the person you think I am. You don't know me. Not really."

"I know you, Kara, probably better than you know yourself."

"No." She shook her head, her eyes filling with a sadness he couldn't comprehend. "There's something that I've been wrong to keep from you."

His heart shuddered. He should have seen this coming. "You're marrying that Spence guy, aren't you?"

Confusion flitted across her features. "What? No. He's not the kind of man I'd ever want to marry."

Relief shot through him. "Then what?"

She wet her lips and he could feel her hands trembling in his. "I know who started that fire twelve years ago."

He frowned, not sure what this had to do with what they'd just been talking about. He'd tried for months to discover who'd started the fire. Got nowhere. Had given up. "How'd you figure it out?"

"I didn't have to." She lowered her gaze, as if with shame. "I've known all along."

"What are you talking about?"

She looked up at him again, her eyes searching his. "I've known who set the fire all along, Trey. Even before you were arrested."

This didn't make any sense. He tried again to pull away, but she tightened her grip.

"Someone confessed to me. I promised not to tell. But I didn't know when I made that pledge that you'd be blamed."

"I must be some kind of dimwit, Kara, but I don't understand any of this."

He finally pulled his hands free of hers, trying to get his head around her words. She'd known who set the fire even before he'd been accused? Is that what she was confessing?

She'd apologized the night he and the girls camped out at the Warehouse. Asked for his forgiveness for leaving him to the law. He'd given it to her—willingly—when he thought she hadn't come forth because he'd rejected her. But she'd lied to him?

His memory flashed to the times she'd tried to talk him out of pursuing his investigation. Tried to convince him he'd do himself more harm than good. He hadn't understood her adamant stance. Now it made sense.

"So a promise trumps truth?"

"Yes. No. I mean, I vowed from the time I was thirteen that unlike my dad, who said he'd always be there for me, I'd never break a promise. I made a stupid, stupid mistake. A mistake you've paid for. It was a decision, Trey, that I've regretted with every breath I've taken since that night."

Her eyes begged for reassurance. Comfort. But even as compassion attempted to claw its way to the surface, still reeling from the shock of her confession he had none to give.

"Who were you covering for?" A list of suspects rowed themselves up in his mind. If it was her "friend" Bryce Harding...

She nibbled her lower lip, avoiding his gaze. "You have every right to hate me. I don't even expect forgiveness."

"Tell me who it was, Kara."

She closed her eyes. "Lindi."

He groaned. A cousin who hadn't even hit his suspect list. He'd never have pegged her. Never in a million years.

"She'd found your lighter in the parking lot after a basketball game that week. Intended to return it. But she'd sneaked down the road from her grandparents' place for a smoke, dropped it and didn't get a cigarette extinguished. I'm convinced it was an accident, Trey."

"This news comes a little late, don't you think? Why are you telling me this now? After all this time?"

"Because I can't live with it anymore. God doesn't want me to live with it anymore. Tonight I finally persuaded Lindi to release me from the promise. Or rather God persuaded her." Her pleading gaze never left his. "She says she'll face whatever she has to in order to clear your name. She's already told her husband. And on Monday we'll tell Reuben. You'll get your paperwork signed."

He stared at her. *The woman he loved.* Absorbing her pain. Her grief. Her guilt and shame. He'd forgiven her once before. Before he knew the truth. Did he have it within him to forgive her now? For the reality of such betraying deceit? Her lies.

A breathless pain twisted through him, mind, body and soul.

Why are you making this so hard on me, Lord?

"I'm sorry, Trey," she whispered. "I don't know what else I can say."

He drew a breath and stepped forward to again take her hands in his, certainty welling in his soul. "How about 'I do'?"

Confusion flitted across her features. "I do—what?"

He quirked a smile at her bewilderment. "How

about 'I do take thee, Trey Kenton, to be my lawfully wedded husband'?"

She stared at him, obviously not comprehending a word he'd said. "What are you talking about? I ruined twelve years of your life."

He tugged her in closer, his heart swelling. "Then, darlin', don't you think you owe me not to ruin the rest of them?"

"But—"

He put a shushing finger to her soft, full lips. Lips he intended to kiss just as soon as he could get her to shut up. It wasn't Valemtime's Day, but it would have to do. Seal the deal on a second chance courtship.

His gaze flicked from her mouth to her eyes. "What part of 'I love you' don't you get, Kara? Are you trying to tell me you don't feel the same?"

She stood speechless as Rowdy danced around them, tail wagging. But from the look now glowing in her eyes, he knew for certain what her next words would be.

Epilogue

"What else can I say?" Trey concluded as he forked up another bite of the Diaz wedding cake and winked at Kara from the far side of a towering bride-and-groom-topped bakery confection. "I had to persuade her to marry me so I could get my hands on that sweet '63 Mustang."

"Bet that's not the only sweet thing you want to get your hands on," Pastor Kenton mumbled under his breath. "Premarital counseling starts Monday. My office. Ten o'clock sharp."

Everyone laughed and Reyna elbowed her ministerial hubby. Kara's face warmed. What an ornery brother-in-law Jason was going to make.

She leaned over to Meg who stood beside her, decked out in white satin and lace and looking every bit as beautiful as any bridal magazine photo. "I can't believe Trey made a big announcement right in the middle of your reception. I'm so sorry. I didn't want him to say anything today. He wasn't supposed to take the spotlight off you and Joe."

"Are you kidding me?" Meg hugged her. "I'd have killed you if I didn't hear the news until we got back from our honeymoon. If everyone knew except me."

"But still—"

"No buts. I'm so happy for you both I could just explode. Do you know what this means? You're going to be living in Canyon Springs, too. Remember? You told me not to hold my breath, but my dream did come true! So when's the wedding? And what are you going to do when you quit your Chicago job? Run the Warehouse?"

"No date set yet. We don't want to rush things."

Meg smirked. "Twelve years is rushing things?"

"You know what I mean. But I'll be working at least part-time at the Warehouse until Mom gets back on her feet. Once we're married, we'll probably be living in the apartment above it for some time to come. But I'm also going to check with your teacher pal, Sandi. She once mentioned a paying designer position was open with a regional affordable housing group."

Her friend sighed happily. "Now wouldn't that be an answered prayer?"

Meg's handsome new husband slipped an arm around his wife's waist. "Warnin' you, Kara. Nobody outprays this little lady."

Both women laughed and exchanged a look born of years of friendship. Then as Kara's mother passed by with a pink satin-clad Missy Kenton in her arms, the little flower girl reached out to her. Kara hesitated, then with a smile took Missy into her own arms. The little girl giggled.

"I may be getting off to a slow start with this full-fledged praying business," Kara admitted, enjoying the feeling of the trusting child snuggling in close, "but I think I'll get lots of practice considering what— and who—I'm committing to."

"Now, is that a fact?" Eyes dancing as his gaze skimmed appreciatively over her Grecian-cut maid of honor dress, Trey set aside the fork and cake plate, then made his way to Kara's side.

Her breath quickened as she met his challenging gaze. "You don't think it will require extra help from the heavenly realms to rein you in?"

"Could be, darlin'. Been runnin' loose on the free range for quite a few years." He eyed the family and friends circled around them, a confiding smile tugging at his lips. "Guess you might say I'm her 'cowboys ain't nothing but trouble' nightmare come to life."

He got the laughter he was aiming for.

She shifted Missy, then slipped her free arm around his waist and momentarily pressed her ear to his chest, listening to the rhythm of a heart she loved. She lifted her head and met his smiling gaze.

"I'm thinking that's a nightmare I'm more than ready to handle, Cowboy."

"You think so, do you?" He cast a deliberately doubtful look at those surrounding them. Gave them a comic I-give-in shrug.

Then lowered his head for a kiss.

* * * * *

Dear Reader,

Welcome back to Canyon Springs!

Nestled in the more-than-mile-high mountain country of north-central Arizona, this is a community where ex-rodeo cowboy Trey Kenton longs to settle down. However, his teenage crush, Kara Dixon, can't wait to see the town in her rearview mirror.

Old feelings rekindle, but Kara harbors a guilty secret that can split them apart for good. One wants to call Canyon Springs home. The other wants to hit the door running. One hungers for roots, the other wings. But both must learn that only by trusting in God and following His leading can their hearts be set free to find a second chance at love.

While writing this book, I was reminded of how all too often we build internal walls to protect ourselves from the hurts of life. In doing so, we often build walls between ourselves and God as well. We refuse to see Him, refuse to hear Him. But He's right there. Waiting for us to open our eyes and ears to His presence. To allow Him to draw close and to help us gain a victory over the hard times that come in life so that we may help others.

I know I've been personally blessed when I'm open to following God's leading, which is how I came to know the wonderful readers of Steeple Hill Love Inspired. Hearing from readers of my first book, DREAMING OF HOME, has been such a joy! I hope SECOND CHANCE COURTSHIP touches your heart as well. Please contact me via email at glynna@glynnakaye.com or c/o Steeple Hill Books, 233 Broadway, Suite 1001, New York, NY 10279. Please also visit my website at www.glynnakaye.com.

Glynna Kaye

QUESTIONS FOR DISCUSSION

1. Kara was barely sixteen years old when she made a promise to keep a secret. Trey later challenges her: "So a promise trumps truth?" Would you as a teenager have made the same decision Kara did? Have you ever done something that you later regretted and wished you could have a second chance to "do over?"

2. Trey bore the burden of having few people believe he wasn't responsible for an incident that occurred when he was in high school. Have you ever had a time when you spoke the truth and weren't believed? How did that affect you?

3. How do you think Kara's father's abandonment affected her decision making? Her career choice? Her determination to get out of Canyon Springs? Do you think she was pursuing a dream in Chicago—or running away?

4. How much of Kara's dislike of Canyon Springs was inside of her and had nothing to do with the town itself? Despite his past

experience in the community, Trey looks at Canyon Springs far differently than Kara. Is it possible for people to legitimately "see" the same place or situations differently than others? Why is that?

5. Trey tells Kara: "Seems to me that most people can be about as happy as they make up their minds to be, no matter where they live." Do you agree with that? Why or why not?

6. Trey longs for roots. Kara longs for wings. Trey asks her: "So you see those two values—roots and wings—as polar opposites? They can't complement and support each other?" What are your thoughts on that?

7. Was Kara's mother right to keep the seriousness of her financial situation from Kara? How could this have been better handled on both their parts?

8. Why do you think it was important for Trey to settle down in one place? What do you think was missing in his life because of the transient nature of his growing up and rodeo years? How might that lifestyle have enriched his experiences in a way that, living in the

same place, he may otherwise have missed out on? Have you always lived in the same place? How do you think that shaped and molded you?

9. Both Trey's old girlfriend and Kara let his background convince them he couldn't make a commitment. How do you think that played a part in Trey's doubting his ability to settle down? Have you ever let someone's opinion of you influence your actions or perception of yourself?

10. Do you think Kara was hurting herself more than she was hurting her father by keeping her anger stirred up against him? Kara's mom tells her forgiving and forgetting aren't the same thing. What are your thoughts on that?

11. What did Kara's mother mean when she told her: "With God's help I choose to forgive—not in the past tense 'chose,' but in an active, continuing tense."

12. Do you think Trey was justified in thinking he couldn't settle down in Canyon Springs because of the "shadow" of Kara hanging over it? Have you ever had a time when your

past overshadowed your present and your future? Were you able to resolve that? If so, how?

13. In what ways did Kara and Trey finally have to step out and trust God in order to allow Him to open the doors to a second chance at a lasting love?

LARGER-PRINT BOOKS!

GET 2 FREE
LARGER-PRINT NOVELS
PLUS 2 FREE
MYSTERY GIFTS

Love Inspired®

Larger-print novels are now available...

Love Inspired®
SUSPENSE
RIVETING INSPIRATIONAL ROMANCE

Watch for our series of edge-
of-your-seat suspense novels.
These contemporary tales
of intrigue and romance
feature Christian characters
facing challenges to their faith...
and their lives!

AVAILABLE IN REGULAR
& LARGER-PRINT FORMATS

For exciting stories that reflect traditional values,
visit:
www.ReaderService.com

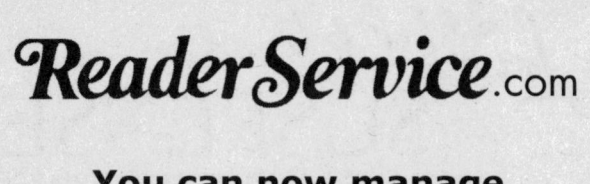